Storm of Desire

The Orion Dynasty Book 4

CK Franco

Blurbs

He's chaos in a billion-dollar suit.
I was hired to tame him.
But storms don't bow to calm.

Orion Vega hides his grief behind scandals, whiskey, and board-room wars. Elara Kent was never supposed to fall for the man she was meant to control.

But when enemies circle and the fight for his sister's future ignites, their collision threatens to consume them both.

Opposites attract. Guardian hero. Passion in the eye of the storm.

To everyone who has ever stood in the eye of the storm—
torn between chaos and calm, grief and hope, fear and love.
This book is for the ones who discovered that true strength
isn't in outrunning the tempest,
but in finding the one soul who chooses to stand with you through it.

"Some storms shatter, others transform—
but even in the shadows of power,
where secrets are weapons and love is forbidden,
there comes one heart unafraid to calm the chaos.
And in that defiance, the tempest finally learns to kneel."

Prologue

The storm began the night his sister died.

Orion Vega stood beneath hospital lights too bright to mourn in, clutching the weight of a single truth: she was gone, and the fragile little girl with tear-stained cheeks was now his to protect. In one breath, he became both guardian and orphaned brother, carrying grief that clawed at his chest like broken glass.

He was brilliant enough to build empires, reckless enough to burn them down, but fatherhood? Stability? Those were storms he had no compass for.

So he drowned himself in chaos—scandals, boardroom wars, sleepless nights where whiskey blurred the edges of his guilt. The world called him untouchable. Inside, he was one misstep from losing the only thing that mattered: Nova.

And then she walked in.

Elara Kent. A woman of rules and reason, hired to bring order to the life he had shattered. She was steady where he was storm, unyielding where he was reckless. She drew boundaries he despised—and yet, for the first time in years, he found himself listening.

Because storms don't ignore the calm.
And calm doesn't bow to storms.

In the shadows of power, where enemies whisper and empires fall from within, Orion Vega will learn that the most dangerous battle is not in the boardroom or the courtroom—
but in the heart of the woman who dares to stand against his storm.

Contents

Scandal Storm

T he city spreads out beneath Orion's penthouse, glass towers snagging the dawn as his phone vibrates with merciless insistence. The walls catch the cold blue of morning; every surface in his lounge seems to reflect a fractured piece of him. His bare feet slide across marble cool as river stones, every step echoing through the cavernous quiet. He stands by the floor-to-ceiling windows, thumb hesitating over the screen, notifications multiplying—red dots like blood blooming across every app. Every ping is a demand, a summons to judgment.

He presses play on one of hundreds of messages. The video fills his screen with brutal clarity: Orion, caught at 3 a.m., staggers from the hush of an exclusive club into a chaos of camera flashes. His hair is wild, his shirt rumpled, stumbling as if the ground has tilted under him. Someone shouts his name—no, barks it like an accusation—and then comes his own voice, too loud and slurring as he jabs a finger at a city official. "Go ahead, call your lawyers! See if they're awake!" The words hang in the air, thick with reckless bravado. Then, the brief, dizzying glare of siren-lit night.

The city's appetite for scandals is insatiable. A single blunder becomes a weapon; reputation is as unstable as the weather. Among these high-rise titans, money isn't enough. Power and bloodlines are nothing if not kept spotless for public view, and guardianship of an heir is a brittle crown, easily forfeited. The board controls not just assets but the definition of family. Their scrutiny does not soften with grief or loyalty. It sharpens, waiting for a moment like this—a slip, a weakness. For those who inherit legacy, an exposed secret, a drunken outburst can erase trust built over generations.

In a mid-morning boardroom clad in frost-pale glass, Ms. Lin—the board's chairwoman—sits at the head of a gleaming table, arms crossed, lips pressed thin. Four members watch grimly as footage of Orion's humiliation repeats, the video's soundtrack of jeers and shutter clicks bouncing against the glass. When it ends, nobody speaks until Ms. Lin's voice, cool as sculpted ice, fills the room.

"I want a complete feasibility report. If Mr. Vega can't fulfill his custodial responsibilities, we proceed—discreetly—toward petitioning for Nova's guardianship." Her gaze lingers a beat too long on the legal adviser, who nods—already calculating. "If Orion won't protect the family legacy, the board will."

Rumors thrive in corporate corridors like weeds in sidewalk cracks. Power shifts quickly here, especially when headlines paint an heir as unruly and unstable. What happens in the city's shadows can poison the boardroom and the household both. Orion's fate echoes far beyond scandal; now it tugs at Nova's very future.

Back in the penthouse, Orion's knuckles blanch as he receives a video call. Shadows flicker across his face as the board assembles on-screen—Ms. Lin's sharp silhouette, the others orbiting her gravity. The air grows tighter, brittle with censure.

"Orion." Ms. Lin's voice rings out, unyielding. "Given your behavior last night, the board is considering a motion to review your guardianship of Nova. This is your final warning. If you wish to retain custody, you'll rehabilitate your public image—immediately."

A dozen retorts flare through Orion's mind, but his tongue feels thick, useless. Ms. Lin's gaze strips him bare, as if cataloging every mistake that has ever stained his name.

"Do you understand the consequences?" she presses.

He nods, jaw tight, unable to trust his voice. He's felt boardroom eyes before: at funerals, at mergers, at the hearing that left Nova's trembling hand in his. Never has their scrutiny stung with such precise cruelty.

A key clicks in the entryway. Caius Drake steps in without ceremony, hair immaculate, suit unwrinkled, eyes already scanning the carnage. The silence bristles.

Caius glances at Orion, then at the wreck of newsfeeds scrolling across every surface. He unbuttons his jacket, not in comfort, but as a ritual—like a surgeon preparing for an operation.

"You need to see what's trending." His tone is steady, but each word lands with intent. "They're mounting a case. Not for business—this is personal. They think you've lost control."

Orion's shoulders twitch. "Let them think it," he mutters, but something fragile in his voice betrays doubt.

"You can't just let it ride." Caius's words are spare, all sinew. "If you don't seize the narrative, they'll hand Nova over and wipe your name from every trust and record. For the board, image is law."

He paces, pulse drumming in his ears. His reflection merges with the city's—hazy midnight hair, haunted eyes, fragments of all the times he's failed to protect anyone. The memory of Nova's small hand clutching his after her mother's funeral aches, a wound stitched with guilt. He hates himself for caring about the board's threats, hates them for holding Nova hostage—but the fear is real, acidic in his throat. Last night was his failure writ large, broadcast for the city to pick clean.

Caius watches silently. No judgment, only cold, unfamiliar pity.

Orion's phone hits the marble with a sharp, splitting crack. The faint tremble in his hands does not go unnoticed by Caius, who steps closer, posture resolute, as dawn sharpens the blue glass all around them.

The soundproof walls of Orion's private study keep the city's afternoon noise at bay, but not the tension that braids through every angled surface. Sulky amber light trickles through slatted blinds, painting sharp shadows across Orion's restless shape as he paces—bare feet scuffing over black marble. The air holds a faint electric tang, the aftertaste of too many tech prototypes and too little sleep, disturbed now by sweat, crushed coffee beans, and the metallic pulse of panic he cannot disperse.

He tosses a glance at the thick door, then turns on Caius with a bitterness that churns hotter for having simmered so long.

"What gives them the right, Caius? One video. One night I forget to be—" Orion breaks off, voice raw. "Now I'm public enemy number one? They think they can treat me like I'm unhinged. Like Nova's some... pawn in their optics game?" His hands knot into fists, restless as caged birds.

Caius, perched on the edge of the bookcase, legs crossed in easy balance, watches him with an inscrutable calm. In this space meant for decisions—shelves lined with technical manuals and old family trophies—he is a still point while Orion's storm gusts unchecked.

With measured patience, Caius's voice cuts through.

"They don't care about last night. They care about the headlines tomorrow—and the custody lawyer they were already calling before noon. That board believes public failure is private failure. If they sense instability in this house, they'll claim Nova needs a safer structure." Caius taps an old news clipping resting by his hip. "I've watched how these stories play. You want to keep Nova? Give them the only narrative they can't attack."

A low, incredulous laugh rips from Orion. "A narrative. You mean spin. Pretend I'm some pillar of virtue, parade Nova on my arm—make the nightmares vanish with press releases?"

"Yes, actually," Caius replies, unblinking. "But not as pretense. Consistency, family, calm routine—that's what the lawyers will look for. I've pulled case files from half the city's billionaire messes. Know what reversed the tides? Showing the courts that someone steady was guiding the home. Not just you. Not some string of nannies. Someone grounded who stays. Nova needs that. You need that." His gaze is steady, nearly gentle.

"I don't need a babysitter," Orion snarls, but his shoulders sag, defiance losing force. His reflection glints, doubled in the glass-topped desk—lines of fatigue carved deep beneath his eyes, jaw shadowed by regret.

"So hire a tutor for Nova. Not for show, but because she needs more than you, and you need—help." The word hangs as if weighted with more than admission. "Someone who can give her what you won't admit you're afraid to provide. Rules. Comfort. Reliability. It doesn't mean surrender, Orion. It means protecting her future."

A thick silence grows between them, the hum of the building's AI controls unheard behind their mutual stubbornness.

"Do you understand what they're circling?" Caius presses, softer now. "They will build a case around every crack. The media, the board, the courts. Even your rivals will send in experts. But nobody can argue with stability."

Orion drags both palms over his tired face, plastering the bite of cold sweat into his skin, leaving red smears on his forehead. The fight is bleeding out of him, leaving only the ache of inevitability behind every belligerent word. He knows Caius is right—knows it in the pit where he stores the old, blistering guilt of his sister's dying wish, where last night's mistakes are only the latest ripples in a storm he refuses to name.

The room feels smaller, thick as a vault. He stares at the window, at the city's spires trussing the sky, all glass and promise—so far below, so easily shattered.

"I can't risk Nova," he mutters, his lower lip trembling before he corrals it with his tongue. "Not just because I'll lose her, but because—" He lets the rest collapse in his chest. Grief can't be said, only survived.

"Then let's start here." Caius opens his laptop, his movements precise and unfazed. The keypad glows cobalt under his fingers, casting eerie light across his determined face. Orion slumps down at the desk beside him, bracing his chin on one hand, only now seeming to notice the way his own pulse beats hard in his ears.

"We'll need someone with discipline," Caius begins, crisp. "Experience with anxious children. Who can stand their ground—Nova's panic isn't just about loss; it's about change. The last few tutors lasted... weeks. Why?"

Orion's jaw flexes. "They broke. They couldn't stop making this about my damn reputation. Or they tried to coddle Nova until she hid in her shell. I don't need an enforcer. I don't need a saint. I need someone... steady. Unafraid to go toe-to-toe with me—someone Nova will trust when I can't get it right."

Caius's lips curve, just barely. "That's the first honest thing you've said since I got here."

Orion snorts, slumping deeper into the chair as Caius scrolls through dossiers built on both expert references and background checks layered with caution. Files flicker across the screen—names, credentials, handwritten notes about boundaries, resilience, and warning signs.

"Composure under fire," Orion adds, eyes scanning the digital haze. "Someone who won't run when the media finds blood in the water."

A short list. Questions rise: How much control does Orion surrender to save what matters most? When does survival require trust?

The printer shudders to life, spitting out the page. It smells faintly of scorched paper and new beginnings. Caius tears the sheet free, offering it—a summons, not an order.

"This is how you fight for Nova."

Orion leans forward at the glass conference table, city lights fanned below like the circuitry of one of his prototypes—ruthlessly geometric, brilliant, unyielding. His reflection swims across the lacquered surface, wavering between rows of digital profiles projected from Caius's tablet. Five faces flicker atop resumes: candidates distilled into summary lines and bullet-point virtues. An ex-principal with a steel jaw, credentials straining under heavy accolades; a gentle-eyed counselor whose file exudes patience; a brisk academic from Oxford, stiff-backed and uncompromising. Fingers tapping, Orion flicks one away.

"Too rigid," he mutters, jaw set.

Caius stands at the table's edge, posture precise. "Rigid can bring order, Orion. Nova's world is chaos. So is yours, in case you haven't noticed."

Pain flashes in Orion's eyes, gone as quickly as it comes. He feigns disinterest, plucking up the next candidate—a former child psychologist who founded a mindfulness academy. He barely reads past the opening paragraph.

"She'll treat Nova like a broken project. That's not happening."

"So you want structure, but warmth. Firm, but not militant. Any other impossible requirements?" Caius arches a brow, unflappable.

"I want someone who'll stay," Orion says, low, almost to himself.

There's a pause. The hum of recessed lighting and the faint vibration of a passing hovercar rise in the silence. Through the window, a storm menaces the horizon—smearing the city's edge in glassy black. Orion's thumbs brush over his cufflinks, restless. Each candidate becomes a mirror for his shortcomings: his volatility, his failure to shield Nova from public spectacle, the ghost of his sister's last, exhausted argument—"You can't always outrun the damage, Orion."

Caius's tone softens just slightly. "We're not looking for someone to fix you or her. Stability, that's all."

Orion rubs the scar on his forearm absently. "We lost stability the day the news started feeding on me. On us."

"Then this is the first step." Caius slides his tablet closer, so the blue-white glow sharpens the lines of Orion's face—a man weighed down, not merely by scandal, but by the slow erosion of hope.

Caius drafts a memo, thumbs gliding over the display. "What do you want to say to the board? I'll keep it simple. You'll look decisive."

Orion's eyes never leave the window. "Say we're taking concrete action. Say Nova's well-being is the only risk that matters now."

They move together before the camera, tension coiling between them. The script is tight: no promises they can't deliver, no hollow speech of redemption. Orion's voice in the recording is steady, but his fingers curl almost imperceptibly against his palm. Even when the message is delivered, its impact bruises him internally—admission, not of guilt, but of responsibility chiseled reluctantly by necessity.

Once the files close, Caius pauses at the door. "Pick someone tonight. Dragging your feet is how the board buries you."

Orion offers only a nod. The door slicks shut; like that, he's alone—cocooned in the blue glow of an office tailored to command but suffocating in solitude.

Night deepens outside, the world gone hush but for the soft whir of the city's monitors scanning for midnight threats. Orion stands pinned against a wall of glass, cool beneath his hands. He traces the moiré of city lights, recalling laughter tucked in quiet alcoves—Nova's giggles, once bright as the starlit skyline. Beneath it, his sister's voice lingers—sometimes scornful, mostly pleading.

You have to want this, she had said. Not for show, not to win, but to keep her safe.

He pictures what could be—a home less haunted, Nova studying beneath gentle lamplight, not leaping at every thunderclap or scandal's echo. If this new hire brings peace, maybe he can finally stop living in crisis mode. Maybe he'd become the man Nova believes he is—the man his sister begged him to try to be.

Or maybe it's another gamble that leaves them exposed, one more stranger marching through his doors, their lives a footnote in a file.

The thought gnaws at him, the old push-pull between running and repairing, the certainty that fate has teeth.

He wipes a finger across the cold glass, smudging the shape of an imagined family.

It's past midnight when Orion finally sheds his armor of authority, the office locked behind him. Barefoot and silent, he pads down the long hall—the air tinged with distant ozone and the faint warmth of lavender. He pauses at Nova's door, opening it with care.

Inside, her room is a hush of dusk blue and gentle white. Nova's breath is steady, her small frame swaddled in the glow of a nightlight shaped like a crescent moon. Plush toys nestle at her side; a sketchbook is half-open on the floor, a field of wild, colorful dreams. Orion approaches—each step slow, his heart thrumming a staccato refrain of fear and yearning.

He crouches, tucks the blanket tighter around Nova's shoulders, smoothing her dark curls with reverent fingers. Her brow relaxes in sleep, unaware of the storms outside these walls.

He whispers, hardly above a breath. "I'm going to do better. For you, pequeña." Not for cameras. Not for the board. For her, for the fragile thread of promise still woven into this fractured home.

Stepping back, Orion lingers in the doorway, his silhouette rimmed in the white-blue glow spilling from the hall. He watches Nova sleep—tiny, unwitting, the center of his universe. The city flickers behind him, full of predatory eyes and silent thunder. Tomorrow, a new force will enter their orbit. He braces for disorder, for hope, for the kind of storm that cleanses as easily as it destroys.

Enter Elara

The elevator doors glide open with a hush that belies the weight of expectation inside. Elara Kent steps out, her back straight and chin tilted in composed defiance. The gold filigree on the lift's interior catches the city lights spilling in through the penthouse's glass walls; it glimmers for a breath before being swallowed by the steely chill of Orion Vega's domain. Her shoes—sensible and unpretentious—mark a deliberate path across veins of white-and-ash marble. The bag in her grasp is practical, an anchor against the vapor of luxury that threatens to swallow substance in this place.

Night presses close against those endless windows, the city unfurling in a mosaic of neon blues and restless reds. The living room sprawls out before her—a pageantry of modern sharpness and calculated calm. Angular furniture, all in slate and soft shadow, lies scattered beneath the vaulting expanse overhead. Fragments of sculpture—glass, metal, ideas made physical—perch atop tables that reflect the shimmering skyline. This room floats above the world but feels untouched by its warmth; every edge is honed and unforgiving.

Orion waits, half-shadowed near the kitchen's slick aluminum counters, where the low hum of hidden machinery barely dares to disturb the silence. He cuts a figure at odds with the intricate serenity—dark hair tousled carelessly, eyes fathomless as the depths of the city. Sinew tenses in his forearms as he folds them across his chest, body language all impasse and warning. The aroma of freshly ground coffee lingers, sharp and smoky, mingling with something colder—an antiseptic cleanliness that marks the air as belonging to someone with more secrets than guests.

"Punctual," Orion says, the word snapped off, each syllable polished and shaped for effect. "Is that the first lesson? Or do you reserve your rigid timetables for children and boardrooms alone?"

Elara meets the bite without hesitation, unfolding herself into the open. She fixes him with a level gaze that doesn't yield to intimidation, only flicks briefly to the piano in the corner—the lone suggestion of vulnerability. Calmly, she slides a paper from her bag, the neat grid of a schedule written by a hand that brooks no chaos.

"I expect structure," Elara replies, her voice even and low with control. "Nova will keep to a regular study rhythm. No unscheduled midnight excursions. She'll have a proper bedtime, and screen time is set—no distractions, no exceptions when it comes to learning." She taps once, crisp, on the page. "If Nova is to thrive here, her environment has to mean stability. That's non-negotiable."

From the shadow of the sofa, a small figure hovers—a girl, barely eight, the city's fractured glow painting her face in patches of blue. Nova has the delicate, wary stance of someone accustomed to reading the air for storms. Her hands twist the hem of her shirt as she studies Elara with wide, uncertain admiration, half-hidden behind a barricade of cushions.

Beyond the glass, thunder mutters somewhere high above the sprawl. In here, the hush is as brittle as bone.

Orion's gaze lingers on Elara, searching for cracks in the calm façade, cataloging the contours of this new intrusion. The gold-and-glass fortress he built atop the city is supposed to keep the world at bay—board members with their threats, news feeds awash in last night's viral scandal, and all the unrelenting greed that stalks his every waking hour. Yet the fortress has become something else: a cage lined with mirrors, every surface reflecting both triumph and the price it claims. Here, privilege is as sharp as the edge of a knife. Here, the lights from a thousand windows can't chase away the encroaching chill of being watched, judged, threatened with the one thing he has no armor against—loss.

He studies the woman determined to chart fixed hours into this chaos, to turn distress into routine discipline, and resents the practicality. He resents how part of him wants to believe it could work.

Nova, unused to this charged dance of adult posturing, shifts from foot to foot. Her mouth wavers toward a smile, not quite daring to form. The thin whorl of her breath fogs the glass briefly as she peeks toward Elara—the tutor who stands uncloaked by wealth or fear, whose words don't bend to stormy tempers.

Orion's shadow wavers across the marble as he steps between the kitchen and the heart of the room, close enough to smell the faint citrus of Elara's soap, to see the steadiness in her eyes that refuses to flinch. In a home where the boundaries are made of steel and secrets, a stranger draws new lines with nothing more than a schedule and a certainty he can't decide if he despises or desperately needs.

"So that's your pitch," he mutters.

"My promise," she returns, unfazed.

In the hush that follows, Nova's eyes dart between them as if searching for the signal that means it is safe to hope. Orion glances from Elara—unyielding and real—to his niece, weighing the scale as silence tightens.

The room holds its breath, and the promise of conflict sparks along every polished surface.

Sharp city lights cut through the encroaching dusk, glinting off the angular glass and steel in Orion's penthouse and splintering across marble floors. Shadows lengthen against the black shelves that cleave the living space, flickering blue accents humming low above the hush. The air brims with the scent of freshly ground espresso clinging stubbornly to metallic surfaces—beneath it, something sharper, the faint ozone tang of a brewing storm beyond the glass.

Orion stalks between the stacks of thick tomes and his territory of the sitting area, restless as a caged animal. Every stride is calculated, shoulders squared and jaw locked in irritation. He watches Elara with a predator's stillness, daring her to blink first. Her canvas bag sits untouched by her side, its neat edges an intrusion—another order imposed on chaos. He lets a brittle laugh break the quiet.

"So that's it?" His voice slides across the marble, laced with acid. "We're meant to pretend this place is a school lab now? Nova's not some fragile machine you can calibrate with a clipboard and a set of standardized checklists."

Elara doesn't flinch. She plants one hand on the back of a low leather chair, facing him with the composure of a woman who expects storms and refuses to yield. Her gaze is steady, dark and undaunted, the light from the windows painting shadows across her cheekbones.

"Nova's routines aren't negotiable," she says, her words precise as cut glass. "She is a child, not a tech patent or a boardroom presentation. Her stability comes first. Under my care, distractions don't set the rules—her well-being does."

Their words snap like live wires. The city glows behind the glass in impatient pulses.

Orion prowls closer, hands flexing—an old impulse to grab control before it slips away. Even now, the world claws at him from every angle: a viral scandal, board members sniffing for weakness, the familiar undertow of loss he cannot patch with code or money. The penthouse, his fortress, now feels brittle. He suspects—no, he knows—that his grip on Nova's world is as tenuous as the shifting skyline.

"You have no idea what you've signed up for," he bites out. The veneer of his voice cracks, revealing something raw beneath. "My life isn't defined by neat calendars and lesson plans. Emergencies don't consult Nova's bedtime before they come crashing in. You really think you can tame this—" he gestures broadly, a sweep of marble, shadow, and sky "—with your rules?"

Elara's fingers curl tighter around the chair, but her expression doesn't so much as flicker. The cool air vibrates between them.

"Your unpredictability is exactly the problem," she responds, her tone a calm rebuke. "Nova is not a variable in your chaos experiment. She needs order and continuity. That's what I'm here to offer. If you intend to undermine that—if you prioritize your routine over hers—then perhaps that's why people question whether you should be her guardian at all."

For a heartbeat, silence fractures everything else—just the low hum of the city, the faint tap of rain beginning to pepper glass higher above them.

Orion's reply dies unformed, caught between indignation and something jagged, shameful. He turns his head away, but not far enough to break the magnetic pull of her stare. He feels the weight of every mistake, each reckless headline, all the late nights when Nova drifted alone on the edges of his busy life. When did he become the problem? He wants to shout, to order her out—for her rules to vanish like the smoke of last night's scandal.

But he doesn't. Instead, he lingers on the precipice of saying too much, the words acidic in his throat. He is not the monster they paint in the news feeds—he is still the boy who once promised his sister he'd never let Nova feel abandoned. But the world keeps taking, and so he takes back, harder, just to survive.

Across the room, Elara remains unyielding; her silhouette is a line drawn in sand.

Outside, thunder murmurs distantly, a prelude. The walls of the penthouse shimmer with city lights and the pulse of machines, yet inside, there's only the thrum of two wills colliding—chaos against order, freedom against sanctuary. It's almost easy to imagine them as adversaries on some forgotten battlefield, each refusing to lower their sword.

Their standoff is a crucible, not just for power, but for the future shape of the family within these walls—a calculated storm that promises to remap every fragile boundary.

In the wedge of silence that follows, Nova drifts into view from the shadows near the hallway, her hand fluttering unconsciously at the hem of her shirt, eyes wide and uncertain. She hovers, the tension crackling around her like static, unsure if she's meant to be a bystander or a casualty. Neither adult moves or blinks, caught in the crossfire, as the city outside flickers and the tumult inside finds no resolution.

Nova's socks make no sound against the marble, but in the hush after the bruise of argument, her presence shimmers—a flash of nervous hope in a world of hard edges. She drifts from the shelter of the low-slung sofa, clutching a bright green notebook tightly against her chest. The city's lights press close on the other side of the penthouse's glass walls, braiding patterns of gold and blue across her face as she stops mid-room, uncertain, blinking up at Elara.

"Miss Kent?" Her voice is a feather's brush, uncertain but bright. "What... what will we learn?" She stands small beneath the ceiling's expanse, her shirt twisted at the hem in anxious fingers, her gaze darting from Elara's face to the silent figure brooding near the kitchen. Shadows puddle around her, but her eyes carry more wonder than fear. Tonight, anticipation wrestles with habit—she has learned to stay invisible, but now she chooses to step forward.

Elara lowers herself to one knee, her canvas trousers whispering against polished marble. The act shrinks the gulf between adult and child, making the city's glass towers outside seem distant and meaningless. In Elara's posture is a deliberate softness that kindles at the sight of Nova's trembling hope. She gives a careful smile, one that gathers Nova into the safety of its warmth, pushing the adult tension into the periphery. "We're going to read about galaxies and measure the speed of shadows." Her fingers tap the side of the bright green notebook, inviting Nova to share it. "We'll build paper bridges and test which ones hold the most marbles. Or maybe," her tone grows conspiratorial as she lowers her voice, "we'll figure out how to make a storm in a jar—just a small one. For science."

Nova's eyes go wide, as if the penthouse itself has suddenly dropped all pretense of threat and invited her in. "Can I show you my treehouse drawing?" she asks, her voice no longer hiding. It's not an offering made to just anyone. She unsheathes her notebook's page—a burst of color and awkward lines, a small fortress suspended in leafy green, a place safer than all the glass-and-marble opulence money can conjure.

Elara doesn't hesitate, accepting the drawing as if it is a treasure map. "Did you design it? Tell me more." She sits cross-legged now, her suit abandoned for a posture that says: I am here in your world, not above it. Nova kneels beside her, their shoulders just touching, the notebook open between them. Crayons have blurred a window yellow, a tiny blue bird darting across.

"The ladder is so nobody falls. And there's space under the branches for my hermit crabs," Nova says shyly, pointing out each imagined detail. She glances up—seeking approval or perhaps something she herself can't define.

Elara gestures to the crumpled edges, the painstaking care of each color, the little bird. "I think this is brilliant. You thought of everything. Maybe tomorrow, we'll map out what kind of tree this would need to be. There's a book on sycamores in my bag—should we look at it together?"

Nova nods, first tentative, then eager. "You know about trees? And storms?" She pulls the drawing closer, almost possessive. The hope that sparked in her voice warms to a laugh—the kind that rarely visits this penthouse since her mother's passing.

Across the room, Orion stands apart—arms crossed, eyes slashed with uncertainty. The dog, sensing quiet, resettles near his feet. Orion's gaze moves like a storm cloud: from Nova, open now in ways he rarely coaxes forth, to Elara, her own reserve visibly slipping. For a moment, he seems caught between admiration and a bruised kind of jealousy. The sound of Nova's laughter is unfamiliar, and he can't quite decide if it's a marvel or a threat. His world, always defined by control, now pulses to a rhythm he does not shape.

Their eyes meet over Nova's bent head, a silent volley. Elara's look is gentle, accepting her place beside this girl—if only for the evening. Orion's is more brittle, the muscle in his jaw tight, his fingers drumming against his sleeve. A question simmers, unasked, in the space between them: What happens when Nova's loyalty isn't his to claim alone?

Time stretches, the city pressing closer as dusk turns blue-black at the windows, and silence washes delicately through the living room. For the first time since she entered, Elara lets herself rest her palm briefly on Nova's shoulder, feeling the small shiver of surprise and then the child's almost imperceptible lean into the touch.

"I want to do the storm in a jar," Nova declares, her notebook hugged tight, her voice small but certain.

"We'll make it our first project," Elara promises, matching her seriousness, her rules, for once, bent in favor of wonder.

Nova settles at Elara's side on the floor, mapping imaginary routes for storm clouds and tree branches on crumpled paper. The city outside sparkles, but the real gleam is here—a hush of fragile hope, a warmth blossoming in the glass-and-marble heart of the penthouse. Orion hovers at the perimeter, a sentinel out in the cold. For the first time, he is no longer the sun around which Nova's world orbits. Even he cannot ignore the shift—subtle as starlight, inevitable as rain.

Tensions and Trust

The penthouse is all glass and storm-blue shadows as dusk creeps up the windows, leaving faint reflections scattered over the marble floors. Nova sits on the living room rug, legs folded tightly, head bowed, clutching her small arms with trembling hands. Each breath comes thinner, sharper, as if the air itself is slipping beyond her reach. Her knees draw upward, knuckles stark against her sweater, eyes wide and unfocused.

A pencil drops from her shaking grasp, spinning in a lazy arc across the rug. Elara is at Nova's side in an instant, shoeless steps barely whispering against the marble. She crouches, her voice pitched soft and careful, the words shaped for a startled fawn rather than a child.

"Nova. Look at me, sweetheart. Take a breath with me. Let's do it together, nice and slow."

Nova's chest flutters—ragged, urgent. She tries, her mouth opening in a soft, keening sound, but panic has already gathered behind her ribs, thickening the air. Her cheeks glisten with sudden tears. Elara's hand finds hers, steady and grounding, her thumb tracing a silent rhythm on Nova's clammy palm.

In the reflection of the window, Orion's silhouette stands locked and towering above the sofa—a statue bristling with helpless fury. His fists flex and curl. He looks as though he's about to break the silence with a roar or shatter the nearest table just to make the panic stop. But he remains there, motionless save for the tic in his jaw, his eyes glued to the scene unfolding at his feet.

"Nova, love," Elara murmurs, searching for Nova's gaze. "We're right here. Nothing bad is going to happen. Focus on my hand. Count with me." The words slip over the choppy rhythm of Nova's breathing, but the child remains trapped behind the glass of her panic—seeing faces, sounds, movement, but unable to reach them.

Elara fumbles for her phone, swiping it open with a muted, muttered curse that she hopes Nova doesn't hear, her thumb seeking Darius's name by instinct born of too many anxious afternoons. She keeps her voice measured as she speaks. "Darius, we need you. Now. It's bad."

The minutes spill like syrup—slow, suffocating, each tick making the air heavier. The room smells faintly of ozone and cleaning products, cold steel and trace perfume beneath the more immediate, living scent of Nova's fear.

Then, the penthouse door slides open with a whisper of hydraulics, and Darius moves in—a wall of calm in dark wool, his eyes gentle but unwavering. He crosses to Nova, dropping smoothly to his knees, pitching his voice to match the gentlest autumn wind.

"Hey, Nova. I'm here. Can I sit with you?" His words hum in the charged silence, never crowding her.

Elara kneels opposite, tightening her grip just enough so Nova knows she's anchored. Darius's large hand drapes across Nova's back, steady and unhurried. "Let's try something easy, okay? Can you listen to my voice?" He guides her: "Breathe in with me. Good...now out. That's it. In... Hold it... Out."

Elara breathes along, letting her own heartbeat slow, her own nerves unwind even as Nova's panic claws at the room. She keeps her eyes soft and her spine unbowed, projecting confidence she fears is only a thin mask stretched over uncertainty. Her mind rakes through every piece of advice she's read, every expert's gentle admonition, compiling it into a script that somehow never feels quite right, because all the science in the world doesn't fill the chasm of watching a child unravel.

She glances toward Orion. He looks ready to shatter—wrung out by the helplessness, hating that his presence isn't enough. For all his power, all his brilliance, he cannot rescue Nova from this invisible threat. The tension crackles between them, silent but dense: Elara's measured calm layered over Orion's electric distress. In their shared concern, there is a strange alignment; the usual undercurrent of argument replaced, for just this moment, by a raw, unguarded fear.

Nova's breathing lurches, hitches. Then, beneath Darius's coaxing and Elara's steadiness, it begins to slow. She speaks in whispers—soft numbers, following the count, clinging to it like a rope thrown into churning water.

Darius's eyes meet Elara's over Nova's bowed head—a communication without words: You're doing all you can. They shift their focus to Orion. Darius nods, barely perceptible, a silent command for patience that the billionaire is poor at obeying. Still, Orion's crossed arms fall to his sides and his jaw unclenches. He doesn't speak, but the atmosphere shifts, ever so slightly—less combative, more protective, all unspoken truce.

When Nova steadies, Darius asks quiet questions: what Nova did at school, when she last ate, what upset her. Elara answers, her voice low and colored with threads of blame—she should have noticed Nova's exhaustion after math, should have softened her words when Orion came storming into the lesson. Each answer is careful, honest, the truth woven with regret.

Darius praises Nova with a smile. "You did well. You're safe. Remember that." He stands, gives Nova's shoulder a gentle squeeze, and meets Orion's worried eyes with a steady promise. "I'll check in soon. Keep things calm. Routine. Elara, journal everything. It helps."

Orion just nods, tension draining, his chest rising in a measured breath he had not found until now. Elara, still kneeling, eases closer to Nova's side. The room, raw and silent, holds them all—wary and uncertain, but, for a moment, together against the storm.

Sunlight pours through tall windows, pooling in warm ellipses across the honeyed wood of the café floor. The air is redolent with citrus peel and steamed milk, the soft hush of morning cut by the occasional chime of the barista's bell. Outside, the city hums beyond a haze of glass, but in here, there is sanctuary—a world pared down to a corner table, ceramic mugs, and a rare unclaimed hour.

Elara's hands are cupped around her mug, fingers curled so tightly her knuckles bear pale crescents. The tea tastes faintly green, grassy, throat-cooling; still, her nerves buzz like static beneath her skin. Lila sits opposite, her posture eased, dark hair swept up, a phoenix tattoo just visible where her wrist rests against the tabletop. Lila doesn't fidget or rush Elara with questions. She simply waits, kind eyes fixed, mindful of the pauses between words.

"I know I should be grateful I get to help her. Nova—I mean. But yesterday... I felt so small, so useless. It's like trying to hold back a storm with my bare hands. And every time I try to set boundaries, Orion just finds a way to blow through them." Elara's voice is rough with the effort of keeping it steady. She draws in a breath, her shoulders tight. "He acts like my routines are for me, or a punishment for him. Not for her at all."

For a moment, only the clinking of a spoon fills the silence. Then Lila leans back, her expression softening with understanding. She turns her mug in slow circles, considering. "When I met Darius, it was walls everywhere—rules, secrets, pain nobody talked about. The Brotherhood runs on loyalty, but trust... trust is slow, and sometimes you swallow loneliness for months before someone lets you in. I kept showing up anyway, even when it felt pointless." Her lips twitch in a faint smile. "Turns out patience and stubbornness are a kind of magic. The more I held on, the more space they offered for healing. I wish someone had told me it wasn't about being perfect, just present."

Elara's gaze blurs. The weight in her chest lifts for a beat, only to settle again, a different ache now—one that hums with fatigue but also glimmers with stubborn hope. She stares at the swirls of tea, blinking back the urge to retreat. "What if showing up isn't enough? Sometimes I feel invisible in that penthouse. I could shout and no one would hear. I keep wanting to fix Nova, as if I could erase her fear with the right checklist, but mostly I feel like I'm the intruder—there but not belonging, like a guest overstaying a welcome that was never offered. Some nights, I count the hours until morning because I can't sleep with all the doubt running circles in my head."

Lila's hand finds Elara's, warm skin against trembling fingers. "You're not invisible to Nova. And you're not failing. Orion's just not ready to trust someone else with his heart, not after what he lost. Consistency is what matters. She'll notice if you keep showing up, even on bad days. Nova needs steady, not perfect. So does he, if he ever lets himself admit it."

Elara laughs, the sound brittle at first, then breaking into a gentle, wavering sigh. "He makes everything a fight—even kindness sounds like a challenge from him."

Lila's eyes dance with knowing. "Orion fights what he can't control, especially feelings. The more you press, the more he'll rebel—it's not personal. I used to keep a list of all the things Darius did that made me want to scream. Then I realized he was as scared as I was, just not good at showing it. With these men, trust isn't a door you walk through. It's a bridge you have to build, plank by wobbly plank, while the wind tries to knock you off."

"He thinks I'm the problem," Elara says quietly. "That my insistence on routines is smothering her. But without them, Nova unravels. I'm terrified I'll do something wrong and... break her."

"You won't," Lila says firmly. "Let her have small choices—what to read, when to rest. Show her the world is safe, predictable. Let Orion see he doesn't have to be the only protector. And when you feel alone, lean into the sisterhood. You're not carrying this by yourself."

They sit for another minute, sunlight crawling higher along the tabletop. Elara turns Lila's words over in her mind, exploring the fragile line between isolation and belonging. The first week in the penthouse, she'd crafted schedules, colored charts, plans with contingency after contingency—old habits built for lonely apartments, substitute classrooms, her heart set on order as a stand-in for belonging. She'd watched Nova spin in panic, Orion rage and retreat, feeling her own voice dissolve amid the wealth and empty space. She'd wanted—needed—a guarantee that love could be engineered, that family could be coaxed from chaos if she just worked hard enough.

But perhaps belonging is something sewn together, one patient morning at a time.

Elara drains the last of her tea, its heat lingering. Lila stands and wraps her in a firm, grounding hug. "You're doing better than you think, Elara. Keep going. Nova—and Orion—they both feel it, even if they don't say it out loud."

Elara nods, a small smile tugging at her lips, resolve threading itself fresh through her spine. "Thank you, Lila. I'll do whatever it takes." She steps into the gentle crush of city noise, the echo of Lila's faith fortifying each step toward home.

Orion leans against the cool edge of the kitchen counter, arms crossed, gaze fixed on the city's dusk-lit sprawl beyond the glass. The penthouse glows with indigo and cold white, the electrostatic hum of concealed LEDs an undercurrent to voices raised, clipped, and increasingly tense. He finds Elara at the other end of the marble island, the new daily schedule clenched between her capable fingers—neat blocks filled: breakfast, reading, art hour, quiet reflection, bedtime routines. The ink is too orderly, too uncompromising, as if a few lines could keep the storm at bay.

"Rigid rules aren't going to fix her, Kent," Orion snaps. "She's not a blueprint or a—damn machine. Nova needs air, not a prison."

Elara doesn't flinch. "Darius said structure would help. Yesterday's panic—"

"You want to turn the place into a prep school? You think that's what Nova wants?"

She holds his stare, her voice maddeningly even. "I think stability matters more than chaos. And she matters more than either of our egos."

"She matters more to me than anyone," Orion growls, his voice flaring, hands splayed in frustration. "I just refuse to see her suffocated."

A beat of silence stretches between them, brittle as spun glass. He studies Elara's expression, looking for any sign of triumph—there's only resolve. Not gloating. Not relenting. "I'm not here to sabotage you, Orion," she says softly. "I'm here because that little girl trusts us to keep her safe. Whether you like my methods or not."

He throws up his hands and storms toward the living room, energy pinging off the sharp lines of glass and chrome. Even as he distances himself, anger uncoiling tight in his chest, he can't shake the biting chill of powerlessness: his fortress penthouse, more of a gilded cage than ever.

He glances back—catches Elara kneeling now, her skirt puddled on the marble, Nova pressed close at her side near the wall of windows. The city's afterglow silhouettes them, and for a fleeting second, the cavernous room feels smaller, almost warm. Elara lets Nova shuffle through a box of colored pencils, her hands moving gently—praise soothing in her voice, steady and genuine. Nova's tension eases, if only fractionally.

Something inside Orion shifts—resentment twisting, not vanquished but changed. He can't dispute the proof in Nova's slackening shoulders or the softness edging Elara's words. He remembers his own sister like this, making order out of chaos with a single look.

He rubs a knuckle along the scar on his forearm, pulse jerky beneath his skin, thoughts stuttering—Is this what letting go of control feels like? Or is it surrender? He's never known the difference.

Nova creeps over, clutching something in her fist—an object mis-shapen, creased by nervous fingers. She presses it into Elara's hand without a word, her eyes wide, flickering with a fear that's more mature than eight years ought to know.

"Sweetheart? What's this?" Elara asks quietly.

Nova's voice is a whisper, thready. "Found it in my backpack at school. It was just... there."

Elara smooths the crumpled paper. Orion sees the black slashing print from across the room, the words thick and unnatural against the white: The Brotherhood's glass towers will crack. Protect the child if you can.

The world narrows, sound flattening to a low roar behind Orion's ribs. He closes the space between them in three quick strides. Elara's thumb hovers, still, over the chilling message, Nova hunched tight against her side. He forces himself to read the note again, slowly, every inch of glass and marble around them suddenly feeling exposed, transparent, breakable.

"Let me see that," he murmurs, his voice sanded rough with alarm. He takes the slip, studying it for signs—no signature, no mark. The city's drone is indifferent, uncaring, pressing in through the glass as if to remind him how high the fall from this place would be.

Nova's hair smells of lavender shampoo—Elara's hand curls around her shoulder. Orion crouches, bringing himself level, careful not to touch, not to frighten. "Nova. Did anyone give this to you? Did you see who put it there?"

A shake of her head, slight and desperate. "No. Just found it after art."

He turns the paper over, searching for anything coded or hidden. Nothing. Just threat, sharpened to a point.

Elara whispers, her voice trembling near Nova's ear. "You're safe, sweetheart. We're right here. No one's getting past us."

Orion and Elara share a look—hers full of cautious strength, his bristling with fear and something rawer, a reluctant trust. A wordless vow passes between them. The air is dense with electricity, the penthouse's illusion of security punctured.

His mind spins: Is this the Helios specter Darius warned of? Have the cracks begun already? If the Brotherhood's glass towers shatter, it won't only be Nova's sanctuary lost, but all his painstaking efforts to protect what little family remains. In the spectral glow of evening, Orion's understanding shifts again. He'll need Elara—her order, her fire. This isn't a storm he can outrun or outthink alone.

They stand like that for a moment, all three huddled over a slip of paper that feels heavier than any weapon. The city pulses beyond, daring them to blink first.

Shadowed Warnings

Night crowds in on the glass-and-steel citadel perched high above the city, a dark velvet curtain studded with distant constellations. Orion Vega strides into his private study, the door hissing shut behind him and sealing away the muffled thrum of city traffic far below. The penthouse's uppermost room is half shadow, blue LED strips casting a cold gleam across the marble floor and black shelves. He drops his leather bag carelessly onto the angular, low-slung sofa—its frame catches a sliver of city light and flares an electric blue at the edge. With a muffled groan, Orion pinches the bridge of his nose, his thumb tracing the half-healed mark beneath his watch strap, the scar a tactile reminder of recklessness that was once survival. In this cocoon of glass and gleaming chrome, fresh from a day spent dueling a boardroom's wolves and dodging commentariat knives, he steels himself for the next gauntlet: the rigid order of Elara's routines, the soft weight of Nova's dependency.

He sits at the wide glass desk, every line sharp and severe as his thoughts. The ambient temperature dips low, making his skin prickle.

He drags a hand through his tousled hair, pressing at the ache building behind his eyes. The tablet—his own design, its shell matte and fingerprinted—wakes at his touch. Notifications flicker in the periphery, but one—crimson and pulsing, not corporate, not casual—splits the screen. No sender, only an address string known to a handful within the Brotherhood. The subject blinks: "Encrypted. Urgent." Orion's heart hammers a little too hard. He glances once at the closed door, then, not quite trusting, a second time.

He enters his access passphrase. The device's speakers click as if swallowing. The lines of code cascade until a single message resolves, razor concise: Watch the shadows in your own house.

A beat of silence pulses. Orion's reflection stares up at him from the tablet—thin, drawn, more haunted than he admits. The words scrawl themselves behind his ribs, cold fingers beneath his skin. He tastes metal, the ghost of blood from too many nights spent chewing at worry. Another trick? Or a threat with teeth sharpened for him alone?

His fingers tremble—so slight that only he notices—as he summons his custom decryption tool. Blue light floods his face. The decryption is fast; Orion's not waiting for protocols tonight. The watermark on the encryption is Brotherhood: the right sequence, the idiosyncratic marker Caius once explained, so subtle that only a handful on earth could spot it. No malware. No phishing. Only intent—calculated, surgical, personal.

Who? For a moment, a gallery of faces parades through his mind's eye—trusted staff, childhood friends, the tight-lipped associates who come and go beneath thick NDAs and heavier glances. Elara, sharp with her boundaries, her discipline etched into every syllable. Nova, vulnerable and trusting, flinching at conflict; barely a suspect, but in a world that bleeds family secrets, innocence offers no sanctuary. Brotherhood. Years ago, there was a breach—papers leaked, a name lost to public slaughter. Orion's hands still remember the tremor of betrayal, the aftertaste of trust snapped in half. Since then, he's barricaded the fragile core of his world with algorithms, cameras, and reinforced glass, but danger is never so basic as brute force.

He breathes out, slow and controlled. What does it mean—shadows in your own house? The phrase loops, squirming. Is it a warning of imminent danger, or a nudge—search here, inside your fortress? Improbable, yet paranoia is a virus, and he has been far too exposed. Perhaps the source is within the Brotherhood itself, someone compromised, someone drawing enemy eyes across the threshold. Perhaps an assistant, trusted for too long, now repurposed as a mole, or an engineer leaving digital breadcrumbs in exchange for their own safety. Every flicker of memory becomes a possible crack.

Orion's thoughts careen, scenes layering like sheets of storm glass—Nova's anxious glances, Elara's precise corrections, the quiet efficiency of the cleaning crew, the German Shepherd's attentive gaze shifting as if it too senses a tremor beneath the surface. Each person in his orbit is now potentially a vector.

He closes his eyes. The city outside pulses with electric possibility, the skyline fractured into fields of gold and icy blue. He's supposed to own this view—command it—yet tonight every reflected shard is a reminder of what he cannot oversee. What if the next cut comes not from the enemy outside, but from within? What if his family, drawn so tight around him, is only here to learn his flaws and sell him for parts?

He snaps the tablet off—a move more final than necessary—and stands. The air in the study carries the clean note of ozone, tinged with the bitter aftertaste of worry. Orion drifts to the window, floor-to-ceiling glass rendering his shape a double exposure: the real man, shoulders heavy, and his spectral outline caught in a thousand city lights.

Fragments of old betrayal gnaw at his certainty—nights spent rebuilding escape plans, the way faith, once shattered, never repairs smoothly.

He watches the shadows slink between skyscrapers, their trails impossibly long. His own reflection gazes back—split and dimmed, a guardian fortified by technology and fear, yet, irreducibly, alone.

Dinner comes late, the city sprawled in electric constellations beyond the penthouse glass. The kitchen's sleek lines gleam under chilly LED track lights, every surface—marble, steel, glass—mirroring their shapes in faint blue gradients. Nova sits quiet and small at the table's edge, her feet swinging above the polished floor, the plush rabbit awkward in her arms. Elara pours soup into white bowls, her movements precise, the air tinged with rosemary and black pepper.

Orion drops into his chair, barely concealing the tautness in his shoulders. The stainless fork tings once against the porcelain. He glances at Elara, then at Nova, assessing them both as if danger might spark from any corner. The lights snap—two quick flickers—casting the room into a burst of stark shadow, then humming back to life. The German Shepherd, sprawled at the archway, raises his head, ears rigid, watching his master for instruction.

Orion's hand goes rigid, knuckles whitening around the utensil. Nova straightens, her eyes frozen on the track lights overhead as if expecting thunder to follow. For a beat, no one breathes.

"It's just the grid," Orion tosses out, his voice flat, brushing away invisible dust from the air. He busies himself with his water glass, his tone too sharp to disguise the pulse at his throat. "Happens all the time—this building has more tech than sense."

Elara's eyes narrow. She sets down her spoon carefully. Nova, her appetite evaporated, nudges her chair closer to Elara, bare knees knocking together beneath the table, the rabbit tucked closer to her chest. The tension swells, an unspoken alarm crawling along their skin, prickling behind ears and at the nape of Orion's neck.

The meal drifts in awkward silence. From the kitchen window, the night glints, the city alive and indifferent beneath them. Orion's mind calculates—door codes, glass sensor status, faces of staff and Brotherhood, anyone who might have lingered too long in the hallway. He measures out composure spoonful by spoonful, but the bitter taste of suspicion curdles in his mouth.

"I'll just grab more water," he mutters, pushing back from the table. Glass in hand, he moves not just to the sink, but in an arc—his eyes sweeping the smart-lock panel glowing green by the entrance, the sealed track of the terrace doors, the panel-fitted security display blinking in standby. His footsteps barely echo on marble, each step a search for disturbance, for any sign the warning was more than a digital ghost. The Shepherd shadows him, nails clicking, tail motionless. Orion kneels, his hand brushing the dog's collar, searching for hidden tells.

Nothing. No breaches, no forced update on the system, no digital alert pulsing an alert into his neural implant. Still—he can't let go of the chill at the base of his skull.

When Orion drifts back in, Elara is already stacking dishes with efficient grace. She meets his gaze squarely, silent questions burning in her eyes.

"Did you actually check something, or just circle around?" she asks, her tone steadier than the quartz counter beneath her hands, but laced with iron.

Orion spikes a brow, his mouth set hard. "It's routine. This place is locked tighter than Fort Knox. Seriously, Elara—there's nothing to worry about."

"Are you sure?" Her syllables are measured, crisp. "Because you're acting like someone who expects ghosts to come crawling out of the walls."

He turns away, irritation a visible line down his spine. "You're reading into things. Nova doesn't need more reasons to worry. Neither do you."

Elara's mouth presses thin. "Now isn't the time to keep secrets, Orion. You say you're protecting us, but you can't do it by pretending frustration is a shield. We're not stupid. Nova sees everything."

That name, spoken quietly, makes Nova hug her rabbit tighter and slide even closer along the bench, her head dipped so only her hair is visible under the white glare. Elara's hand hovers above Nova's—close but never forcing.

Orion's jaw works. "I'm not keeping secrets. I'm keeping things functional. There's a difference."

Elara sighs, collecting empty glasses, her tone gentler but not yielding. "Pretending everything is fine—that's what children do when they think the monsters outside will vanish if they're quiet enough. We can't fix what we don't talk about."

"That's easy for you to say," Orion retorts, tension caught brittle in his voice, but Nova flinches almost imperceptibly at the sound.

The hush returns, dense and breathless. The clatter of dishes is overly loud, echoing in the white expanse. Nova retreats so far into Elara's side she might disappear beneath the crook of an arm, wordless, small, the rabbit now a furred talisman.

Orion drifts toward the sprawling windows. The city is nothing but a splintering web of blue and gold. His reflection hovers in the glass—framed by light, but untouchable. Elara lowers herself onto the bench beside Nova, letting the little girl's head drop to her shoulder. In that gleaming, silent fortress, they sit as three distinct bodies sharing a single, uneven breath—the fragile balance of trust, hope, and suspicion trembling with every muted heartbeat.

The evening settles like static, thick with the scent of cooling soup and the electric tang of secrets still unsaid.

City light splinters across Nova's ceiling, caught on drifting motes in the hush just past midnight. Elara stands in the hall, the silence veined with the hum of distant traffic and the low, nearly imperceptible growl of the German Shepherd lying sentinel at the threshold. Then—a faint sound, muffled movement beneath blankets. She edges open Nova's door, letting clean light from the corridor pool at her feet, mingling with the warm, honeyed glow of the reading lamp that guards against monsters flickering at the edge of dreams.

Nova is a small ball of tension on her coral chair-bed, breaths shallow, fingers clamped like iron around her plush rabbit. Shadow ripples beneath her eyes—old, underwater panic. Elara kneels, moving slowly, letting mattress springs whisper her intent. Her hand finds Nova's dark curls—a soft, anchoring stroke.

"Honey? Breathe with me," Elara murmurs, her voice pitched low enough to catch only in Nova's shaken space. "One in, two out. Count with me."

Nova locks her gaze onto Elara's steady, dark eyes. Elara's fingers, cool and reassuring, pace a gentle rhythm on Nova's scalp. The blanket's synthetic softness rustles as Nova tries, her shoulders jumping with each damp inhale, then uneven staccato release. The city's lights flicker yellow-green on their faces, painting the quiet with a strange, otherworldly safety.

Elara hums—a threadbare lullaby passed from her own childhood, notes worn smooth by time and pain. In the sound, there is memory: her own mother's arms around a smaller, breathless girl, a room smelling of salt and ocean air. Grief flows behind the melody, but she keeps it leashed. This is Nova's night, not hers.

"The shadows out there can't reach you," she whispers. "You're safe, right here. Orion's here. I'm here. Nobody's leaving."

Nova's breaths begin to slow, her rabbit loosening in her grip. Elara notices the faint sheen of sweat at Nova's temple, the taste of old fear mingling with the dry air—tonight feels thick as rain that never breaks, heavy with things unsaid. Nova's hands relax. One threads into Elara's.

Down the hallway, a new presence—that peculiar mix of threat and longing he always brings—looms at the threshold. Orion leans on the frame, hulking and out of place in this fragile sanctuary. The streetlight blades him in two: half illuminated, half memory. His arms cross, jaw tight, but his eyes are pools of wreckage, glassy and unguarded. He watches, silent, as if catching echoes of a song he's afraid to hear too clearly.

"She's okay now." Elara's tone is for Nova, but the words float to Orion, a thread thrown out, fragile as spun sugar.

He shifts, weight restless. Guilt radiates off him, thick and bitter. She feels it, wants to push it back at him, but tonight is not for fights or questions. Orion's hands flex uselessly, longing to cross the distance, to fix what can't be solved with money or reputation. Instead, he draws the door halfway closed—his silent admission of trust, or surrender.

As Nova drifts closer to sleep, Elara's mind wanders—back to tear-stained nights in the faded blue room of her childhood, holding a brother's trembling form, whispering promises she was far too young to make. Back to the classroom with anxious students, the quick, prickling terror of panic attacks that never moved in a straight line but always, eventually, yielded to patience and repeated assurance. She knows these storms; she has learned not to fear them, only to weather them, to build levees of routine and gentle presence. It's why she's here, in this citadel of glass and steel and hidden scars, in the orbit of these broken, brilliant souls.

But tending to Nova, breathing with her, she feels the old ache—the sharp awareness of how breakable all of this is. The pressure of expectation from above, the crackling tension with Orion, the certainty that secrets move like cold currents beneath their feet.

She holds Nova's hand long after the child's breathing deepens. The city's noise falls away, leaving only the mechanical hush of air through ducts and the stray pulse of cars passing far below. Between them, the plush rabbit lies slumped, guardian of dreams.

For a while, Elara just stays, watching the door. Through its crack, the glow of the hall shivers faintly—a signal, a wound. She senses Orion still standing nearby, wondering if he's listening or simply unable to walk away. This, too, is a dialogue between them, wordless but impossibly deep.

When she finally bends close, her voice a wisp, she whispers to Nova, "You're safe. I promise. I'll keep you safe. Storm or no storm."

Outside, the penthouse stretches into the hush of three a.m., luminous and still, as if holding its breath for what comes next.

Clashing Worlds

Orion enters his bedroom with the careless stride of a man trying to outrun the day. Fingers flying, he yanks his jacket off and slings it over an angular armchair, the supple leather sighing beneath the sudden weight. The faint shimmer of city lights plays across the floor-to-ceiling glass behind him, fractured by his movement. With a practiced flick, he shrugs out of his shirt—then another—letting them puddle in careless heaps on the cold marble. His shoes scuff as he toes them off mid-stride, sending socks slithering under the bed's low platform. The air carries hints of bergamot and ozone, his cologne mingling with the sterile, metallic scent of the penthouse—a storm barely held at bay behind glass.

He barely notices the way his chaos ripples outward. One corner of his mind registers a half-finished work file still open on the bed's cobalt-blue coverlet, white pages splayed out like wings.

Elara arrives, arms full of towels folded with clinical precision. She stops short, breath stalling as she surveys the battlefield of discarded clothing and open drawers. The sharp angles of the room—steel and glass, harsh and gleaming—look all the harsher for the disorder Orion has left in his wake. Her brows knit together, slashing down in stern lines as she kneels to scoop up a sock. Fingers tight around the fabric, she straightens, the neat stack of towels trembling dangerously.

Another shirt flutters to the marble behind Orion as he moves toward the bed, oblivious. She can taste a bitterness on her tongue; frustration and exhaustion coagulate in her chest, a slow burn.

"Would you mind picking up after yourself?" Elara's words slice through the hush. Her tone is level, clipped. "It's impossible to keep this place livable—much less conducive for Nova's studies—if you turn every shared space into a disaster."

Orion cocks an eyebrow, amusement flickering over his features. "Relax. It's not a boarding school—or did I miss the new regulations?" With a flourish, he collapses backward onto the bed, arms splayed. The sheets wrinkle under him; another shirt flops to the ground at his side.

"That's not the point." Elara's grip on the towels tightens until terrycloth creaks. "She can't focus with this... this chaos everywhere. I'm trying to build something stable for her. If you cared to notice, order helps her breathe right now."

Orion's mouth curves into a lopsided grin—a dare, not an apology. He props himself up on an elbow and regards her, eyes dark with mischief and challenge. "Stable, huh? You mean boring. Sorry, but I don't need every second of my life color-coded for maximum efficiency. Chaos works for me. Always has."

Her nostrils flare in silent retort, irritation coiling low in her gut. The towels tremble again. Her gaze lingers on a child's notebook peeking from beneath the bed—Nova's, left behind in another of the day's small retreats. The sight hardens her resolve.

"Your chaos isn't just yours anymore." Her voice is quieter, armored in steel. "We share this home. Nova shouldn't have to carry your mess, too."

He smirks, eyes glittering. "You sound just like my old headmaster. Maybe next you'll hang a gold-star chart in the hallway."

A hush falls, broken only by the distant hum of the city below. In the doorway, Nova appears—a ghost at the threshold, barely audible. She clutches a battered book to her chest, knuckles pale with uncertainty.

"Um..." Her voice trails off, shy but determined. "Maybe—maybe you could split the closet? And, um, keep the parts we all use clean? I can help if that makes it easier. Then everyone's happy."

Orion and Elara fall abruptly silent, the tension in the room a palpable electricity. He sits up, unruly hair falling into his eyes. Elara's shoulders remain rigid, lips pressed white around a thousand unsaid words. The room's brittle energy halts, suspended in Nova's hopeful gaze.

Outside the window, city lights refract in droplets against the glass—reflecting the precarious balance inside. Silence thrums, held in Nova's anxious expectation.

Under the city's shimmering night, three figures hang poised: one bristling, one wounded, one desperate for peace. The storm between them holds, unbroken.

Elara stands at the edge of the penthouse living room, sleeves rolled just above her elbows. The marble beneath her feet gleams, refracting sunlight that pours through glass walls—a white-hot glow that burns away any hint of drowsy morning complacency. The city sprawls beneath, expansive, unknowable. In here, every inch pulses with artificial order: Nova's desk positioned precisely for optimal light, the bright markers capping a whiteboard whose grid rivals the city's own lattice.

She writes—lavender for reading, teal for arithmetic, orange for break—her script looping with compulsive precision. Each line is a challenge flung at the world: I can impose sense here. Nova watches, small brown eyes framed by dark curls, her body held nearly still except for the restless tap of one foot. The scent of citrus—for focus, Elara insists—lingers above the smell of polished steel and old coffee.

Barely a minute into phonics, Orion drifts through the room. His voice, clipped and electric, rises above the hush like a wrong note: "Yes, send me the schematic—three days, not five. No, ignore Boardman; he panics at shadows." He's a riot of nervous energy in a world meant for calm—hoodie askew, phone pressed hard to his ear, finger swiping furiously at tide after tide of notifications.

Without missing a beat, he paces past Nova's desk, oblivious to the grid of lesson plans. A vibration—notification or just kinetic restlessness—flickers beneath his skin. His eyes—dark, quick, avoiding—register neither the hour nor its purpose.

"Nova, rooftop lunch. Best view in the building, croissants and cloud-spotting. Arithmetic can survive the great outdoors, can't it?" His mouth curves, coaxing mischief from the muted morning.

Nova almost dares to look at Elara, hope and guilt warring on her face. But Elara's marker halts, poised midair. Her tone is unwavering—steel beneath velvet. "No, Orion. The schedule isn't a suggestion. Nova needs consistency, not chaos. This is her school block, and it's not up for negotiation."

He scoffs, not cruel but sharp enough to leave a mark. "What happened to learning through play? Or is this place a boarding school now?"

"A place for learning and for feeling safe," Elara replies, drawing a line beneath the schedule, the air dense between them.

Orion's jaw tightens, but he winks at Nova as though nothing's amiss. He slumps into a low leather armchair and props one scuffed sneaker on the glass table, phone still in hand, his voice slipping to a murmur as he resumes his call. "Some people need monotony, Nova. Me, I need inspiration." There's bravado for show, but a shadow blooms in his eyes.

Resentment and guilt throb under Orion's practiced nonchalance—unseen currents warping the simplest morning. His world, built on the thrill of spontaneity and last-minute innovation, narrows beneath Elara's lines and rules. A lesson plan is more than color and ink; it's a barricade—no space for impulse or escape. Here, in the stark morning blaze, he is a trespasser in his own home.

Nova sits straight-backed, small fingers hovering above the column of equations. Elara coaches her through long division, her voice pitched low and attuned to the tremors in Nova's hands. For Orion, the act is intimate, exclusionary. He scrolls his inbox, each flashed message a jab—reminders of the world outside pressing in, of decisions he'd rather make, freedoms he no longer owns. Through the glass, he watches the city, comforted and threatened by its expanse—by all the roads that lead away from this sterile, ordered morning.

He can't escape the memory of his sister's apartment—messy, bright, forgiving. Nova was smaller then, giggling as she spilled blocks across the carpet, his sister laughing, unbothered. The pang is sharp: he'd promised Nova freedom, love without strings. Yet all he offers now is the shadow of someone else's order, as if safety means containment.

He steals glances at Elara, at her unruffled focus, lips pressed tight. He doesn't doubt her devotion—her intent to heal what's fragile in

Nova. But he resents the way her resolve knocks hard against the corners of his world, driving him out of orbit. And beneath that heat, something unexpected simmers—a reluctant respect, the spark of hunger for structure he's always denied.

Another block: reading. Elara's voice draws Nova close, anchoring her like a ship in wind. Orion understands, in some battered recess of himself, that this is necessary. That order is a kind of love, even when it stings.

"Vocabulary journal, Nova," Elara prompts softly.

Nova's pencil scratches, her eyes flicking upward. "Does 'routine' mean rules that help you...not worry?"

"In a way. They help you feel safe enough to try new things," Elara answers, glancing toward Orion, her gaze direct, challenging.

He closes his laptop, heaviness gathering behind his ribs. At the last word of the lesson, the room quiets. Sunlight shifts, painting a slow arc across the glass and marble. Elara presses the last magnet onto the board—worlds in perfect order—while Orion hunches deeper, scrolling through emails he barely sees, brooding as the lesson ends and the morning's truce dissolves into silence.

A hush lingers in the penthouse, afternoon gold spilling molten through the windows and casting halos across polished stone and shadow. Nova crouches by Elara's office, breath held tight in her chest. Her heart bumps against her ribs as the memory—Orion's voice raised, Elara's clipped retort, her own toes curling into thick carpet in the next room—crowds out all the calm she tried to gather that morning. It's quiet now, but Nova knows quiet is only a pause between storms, and grown-ups can spark lightning with a single word.

She slides her note under the door, a secret offering more fragile than it looks. The paper is folded and soft around a drawing—stick figures of herself, Orion, and Elara holding hands under a blue sky that hasn't been real in weeks. Between them, smiling suns hover, and below, she wrote what she couldn't say out loud: Thank you for helping us. She imagines Elara finding it, her practical hands pausing, maybe a shadow of a smile breaking the worry line between her brows.

Nova tiptoes down the corridor, past the kitchen suffused with the faint scent of cumin and melting cheese. The air is warm, still carrying traces of last night's argument. She stops by Orion's study, a cave of technology humming behind the glass. His laptop glows with lines of code and business graphs, the screensaver flickering. Nova places a charm—a single blue bead threaded on yellow string, knotted imperfectly and smooth from anxious fidgeting—beside his keyboard. She whispers, "For luck." Her voice doesn't carry, but she hopes the bead keeps the restless shadows away better than her locked jaw or silent prayers.

The penthouse stretches with bottle-green dusk outside, but the real wilderness is inside—every room split between places she can curl up and places she's not certain she belongs. Nova gathers her courage, brave in her socks, her pulse thrumming loud as wind against the window. She pads to the living room, the hush so complete she can hear Orion's shoes land carelessly on marble from across the suite and Elara's pen scratching intent lists on smooth white paper.

"Um," she says, voice trembling, her thumb tightening over the spine of her favorite book. "Could we...maybe...play something? I thought, maybe, before dinner? Charades, or a board game, or—" She can't quite look at either of them, so she fixes on the glowing blue beneath the glass coffee table, pulse fluttering in her neck as she waits. Her chest swells with hope and dread—any moment, they might shrug, or sigh, or say not now, and the gap will stare back, wider than before.

Orion looks up first, brows raised, his arm still slung across the back of his chair. For a heartbeat, he's all rough impatience, but when he catches the small shake in Nova's voice, his facade slips suddenly—a flash of old guilt flickering in his eyes. He drags a hand through his unruly hair and arches an eyebrow at Elara. Elara lowers her pen carefully, assessing Nova with that clear-eyed steadiness that anchors her. A shadow of exhaustion passes over her lips, but she nods, much softer than before.

"That sounds like a nice change," she says. "Charades, or something else? You choose, Nova."

Orion stretches, boots thumping to the carpet, reluctant but not oblivious. "Fine. Guess that means I'll have a shot at losing dignity in my own home, huh?" His voice is teasing, gentler in its sarcasm than it would have been yesterday.

Elara flashes him a warning look. "We can keep it fun—and digni-fied. For Nova, at least."

"I'll try. No promises," he mutters, but when Nova glances up at him, a half-smile sneaks through.

The board game box is heavy in Nova's lap as she sits cross-legged on the floor. The polished table beside her is cold under her elbow; her hands shake slightly as she sorts cards, pretending that the rules on cardboard matter more than the rules of the house. Orion sprawls on one side, all kinetic limbs and restless energy, while Elara perches primly across, her eyes trained on Nova for cues. The first round is stiff—Nova acts out "robot" with stiff arms, her mouth in a silent O, but her nerves trip her, and she nearly loses courage until Orion guesses, "Transformer with a flat battery?" which makes Elara stifle a sudden laugh.

Their laughter comes hesitant, punctured by memories of old silence. Nova feels the knot in her stomach ease a little—a firefly flicker of happiness. Each turn draws them minutely closer: Orion gesturing wildly, Elara guessing in deadpan tones, Nova hiding giggles behind her palm. The city beyond melts gold and indigo, neon flickering against the windowpanes as shadows lengthen.

Nova remembers other nights—after the messy kind of shouting, after doors slammed and tears choked behind locked bathroom doors—where she drew herself small and wished for quiet, for togetherness. She clings to this moment, senses sharpened. The tick of the clock is softer, the world's edge blunted by Orion's joking loss and Elara's half-smile. She has no spell to keep this from breaking, but she wishes fiercely, watching their faces soften around the edges. She wants to ask, Can we stay like this? but doesn't say it, because wishing and speaking are different kinds of magic.

On the last round, Orion finally guesses Nova's clumsy crab-walk, and Elara lets herself laugh low and real. For the span of one sunset, Nova feels the family she's pieced together from shards and shadows may yet belong to her, if only until the light fades.

As the final game piece slips back into the box, sunlight painted copper across the glass, silence settles—gentler than before. They sit together, close but cautious, while unspoken tension hovers just beyond the rim of light, waiting for night to draw it in once more.

Night presses its face against the glass, skyscraper lights bleeding into the penthouse living room. Here, shadows cluster in the corners, broken only by the blue glow of Orion's laptop. The drone of keys and the muted threads of city sirens fill the sprawling room, oppressive and relentless.

Elara appears from the hallway, her hair still damp at the temples from the mist of Nova's bath, clutching a towel in one hand. She tightens her robe and pauses—a steady, deliberate breath recalling her own center. She surveys Orion, hunched and intent, the silver light casting hard lines along his jaw, the world on his shoulders and under his thumbs.

"It's bedtime." Her voice is low but unyielding, slicing through the hush.

He doesn't look up, fingers tapping like errant rain against the keys. "You know some of us actually start working after dark," he mutters, his eyes fixed on a column of encrypted code glowing across his screen.

"Nova needs quiet. Routine. You promised." Her hands knot the towel tighter. "Electronics off, winding down. That is what helps her sleep. You said you'd respect that."

He leans back, his eyes dark and glinting in reflected city lights. "I said I'd try. What, you think the world stops spinning at nine because you draw a line in marker and call it a boundary?"

"We're not at a tech launch, Orion. It's not about your groove or mine—it's about her. You can't be unpredictable all day and then expect her to just adapt. She needs calm at night, not more chaos."

He swings his legs off the coffee table, defiance flickering across his face. "You treat me like I'm the problem. Newsflash: I'm her guardian. Maybe this whole bedtime drill is just stressing everyone out. Have you considered that?"

"I treat you like an adult who should know the difference between caring and control."

"And you?" He snaps the laptop shut, the sound sharp as a whipcrack. "You act like your rules are sacred. Maybe you're not as open-minded as you want everyone to think."

A beat passes—long, taut as drawn wire.

"You don't even try to trust me," he says, his voice edged with something raw. "You swoop in, fix everything, rearrange our lives like you're the only grownup in the room."

"If I don't step in, who will?" Elara almost laughs, but it comes out tight as a swallow. "You run from responsibility the moment it conflicts with your comfort. That's not guardianship, Orion, that's avoidance."

His reply is a bark of derision. "Nice. You want deference? Earn it. This isn't a school, and I don't need you policing my every move."

Across the living room, the hum of tension grows louder than the city. Silence swells between them, thick with the things unsaid and unforgiven.

From the dim hallway, Nova appears—a small, frail ghost in a fluffy robe, clutching her stuffed lamb beneath her chin. The hush of carpet muffles her steps. She hovers at the threshold, eyes wide and glassy, shrinking deeper into the plush sanctuary of her toy.

The argument continues, voices sharpened now, old resentments dragged into the light.

"You think giving in would mean losing your edge—but sometimes compromise is the only proof of maturity."

"Spare me the lectures. Maybe I just don't see the world in binary like you. Nova's my family. I get a say, even if you don't approve of how I protect her."

"Protection means consistency, not chaos! She can't sleep when she thinks the world will fall apart at midnight."

"You think she can't see how you hover over her, waiting for her to break? That's not safety, Elara—it's a cage."

Elara's lips part—then close. She looks down at the floor, then up at him, grief radiating in the stiffness of her posture.

Beyond them, Nova hugs her knees, her knuckles white. The living room seems vast, the ceiling impossibly high, silence draping heavy after every jagged word.

Orion's rage fractures; his hands tremble, knuckles gone pale. With a final glare, he snaps the laptop into his bag and stalks out of the room, his shoes echoing on marble. The door to his study slams, vibration humming through the floor. Silence pools in his wake—an unyielding, thick thing, full of jagged edges.

Elara stands frozen, then lets herself drop onto the edge of the sofa. The blanket is soft beneath her hand but offers no comfort. Her heartbeat tumbles, unruly and graceless, her mind swirling. Is it always going to be this—his wild colliding with her order? Every evening a cliff they tumble off, a compromise that shatters as soon as one of them feels threatened or unheard? She pictures Nova, tense in the doorway, learning already that love is something fragile, brittle—something to tiptoe around.

Elara cradles her head in her hands, listening to quiet footsteps fading down the hall. Maybe this house will never settle—a place run by storms, not by reason. Maybe all she can do is keep Nova afloat between tides of chaos and rebellion, forever nursing a hope there's a new beginning waiting, if only the storm ever passes.

Nova lingers by the archway, small and uncertain, the night stretching around her. A family: is this what it's supposed to feel like?

Breaking Points

Morning light sharpens every edge in the penthouse kitchen—a place engineered for calm, now humming with restlessness. The chill in the air collides with the acrid scent of espresso brewing. Elara stands alone, one hand tightly gripping a phone left abandoned on the marble counter. The screen gleams a hostile blue: missed calls stack into the double digits, voicemail notifications glowing red with urgency. It's Orion's work phone, its silence heavy with accusation, timestamps jarring—9:16, 9:22... right through yesterday's mathematics hour with Nova.

She moves through the kitchen, her footsteps a soft rhythm against the stone floor. Orion's back is to her, sleeves rolled, his form outlined by city light streaming past the glass. An electric kettle whirs. He clacks a mug onto the counter—precision movements that try to pose as casual, but Elara can see the nervous energy flowing beneath his skin.

She holds up the phone, her voice clipped. "Are you planning to respond to any of these, or is ignoring everything the new household rule?"

He pivots, his face unreadable save for the sharp set of his jaw. "Can't get to every little crisis. Believe it or not, this place doesn't stop spinning if I don't pick up a call."

"Except these aren't little crises." The phone is set between them, a silent witness. "The board wants answers. Nova's lesson was interrupted three times last night by your partner demanding to speak with you about the European launch. I told him it was after study hours, but he was insistent. This—" she gestures to the device, "—has consequences for more than just your image."

Orion opens the sugar jar with a jerk that rattles the glass. "You tracking my calls now? What else—the number of times I go to the bathroom?"

Her lips press into a thin line. "The only thing I'm tracking is how frequently your choices leave Nova adrift. She barely slept because you barged in after midnight. I found her drawing on her homework at two a.m."

"And suddenly that's my fault?" The spoon in his hand clatters onto the cold marble, echoing off stainless steel. His shoulders square, every muscle tensed—defensive, cornered. "You have no idea what I'm dealing with. You want everything on a schedule—the kid's entire existence planned to the last second. Maybe she needs less rigid structure."

"She needs predictability." Elara's composure is as rigid as the backbone she leans on. "That's the only thing that's ever made her feel safe. Do you even see what last night did to her?"

Orion's stare is hard, yet quivers at the edges. "You're not her mother, Elara. You're not mine either."

A brittle silence. "No. But someone has to act like an adult here."

"My name's on the papers. I make the calls—for Nova, for the company. Not you."

"And while you're playing king of the glass tower, remember who mops up after your storms. Nova is terrified most nights. Is that how you think guardianship works?"

He scoffs—a rough, bitter sound. "You talk boundaries, but all you do is trap us. I have two jobs—keep my company from burning, and keep Nova from shattering. Your rules make it harder, not easier. Some days it feels like you're hoping I'll fail."

"I'm hoping you'll step up." Elara's voice tightens. "I care about Nova's stability more than my job. Get angry with me if you want, but I won't be sorry for doing what's right for her."

"Convenient for you. You get to walk away if this goes to hell. For me, it's family. Or what's left of it."

The soft scuff of slippers halts them. Nova's figure fills the doorway, hair mussed, clutching her notebook like a lifeline. She hovers, wide-eyed, small shoulders bunched defensively as she stares between her uncle and her tutor. Tension bites the air. Elara's heart constricts, guilt mixing with dread.

Orion's hands flex at his sides. He turns away first, his voice thick. "I can't do this right now." He sweeps past Nova, his departure a gust that empties the room of heat. The glass door shivers in its frame; footsteps recede, pounding hollowly into the silence.

Nova stands frozen, blinking behind lashes damp with close-held fear. Elara opens her mouth—closes it. The girl clutches her notebook tighter, then ducks her head and retreats, bare feet nearly soundless against the tile.

For a long moment, all that fills the kitchen is the quiet ticking of the clock and the bitterness of coffee gone cold. Elara braces her palms against the counter, steadying her breath, eyes fixed on the door that swallowed Orion. Nova's untouched breakfast sits growing colder by the minute, a small, silent casualty of the storm.

Orion stalks into his private study, the door thundering shut behind him. The handle vibrates under the force—a futile show of finality in a place where nothing feels certain. He paces, heel to toe across the polished lines of the marble. Glass and steel, reflective surfaces, nowhere to hide. The city pulses silently through the window: cloud-thick daylight glinting off towers, the penthouse high above the hum of consequence. His reflection shivers as he passes, jaw taut, shoulders unyielding.

Each accusation from Elara weaves itself into his thoughts, barbed and persistent. Reckless. Irresponsible. Endangering Nova. Her voice clings to the walls, even as he clings to denial. Orion's fingers drum restlessly on the cool edge of the desk, the gesture sharp, anxious. It isn't that she's wrong—he knows it. But the boundaries she sets feel like shackles. Every minute scheduled, every slip scrutinized, every ounce of control wrenched away from hands already shaking from the weight of guardianship. His autonomy, thinned to a whisper between the responsibilities he can't outrun and the freedoms that kept him afloat.

He yanks his encrypted phone from the drawer beneath a stack of unopened mail. He scrolls quickly, finds Caius's secure line. The city shimmers beyond the window, indifferent to the echo of his frustration.

"She's suffocating me, Caius," Orion grinds out, his tone edged with old hurt. "It's like living in a locked lab—every move monitored, every hour accounted for. I can't breathe. Nova's calmer, sure, but is this sustainable? I can't keep doing this. I'm not built for caged routines and household protocols. It's not me."

The line hums, then softens under Caius's measured voice. "That may be, but the board is watching. Publicly, you're dancing on a tightrope. Privately, the moment you falter, they'll move—take Nova, dangle your missteps out for the world. She is the only thing you cannot afford to lose. You know that."

A muscle jumps beneath Orion's jaw. He slumps against the desk. Boardroom politics, parental sabotage, guardianship as spectacle. The threat of losing Nova has become more than a nightmare—it's a shadow, growing longer with every misstep, every tabloid photo, every heated exchange within these glass walls. He hangs up without another word and stands at the window, hands pressed flat against the cool pane, city breath pressing back at him. Sunlight slides in angled sheets onto the whiskey bottle on the credenza: half-full from the night before, the color deep as unease. Temptation. He turns away and lets it wait, his pulse harsh and ragged. Freedom, he thinks, once tasted like this—sharp and burning, but now it dulls into guilt.

In another wing, Elara perches at the edge of the guest bed. Sunlight curls around her calves, warm but impersonal, a distant comfort. She presses her phone between her palms, thumbs poised over the screen, composing a message and erasing it, over and over again. When Lila's call finally comes, her voice is thin, brittle at the edges from fatigue.

"I don't know if I can reach him," Elara says quietly. "Every time we pull Nova back into the ordinary—school, meals, even sleep—he does something to undo it. Another late-night meeting, another set of missed calls, more chaos. I'm tired. But Nova..." She swallows, her voice shaky but not broken. "She's worth bruising my pride. I can't walk away, not while she's just starting to trust us. Not while he keeps pretending he doesn't need help."

"Hey," Lila's voice is sturdy and warm, a gentle anchor in the tumult. "You're fighting for both of them—even when he can't admit it. He won't change overnight, but you have to keep your line. You're the only one who tells him the truth, Elara. Don't let him push you out because it's hard. I'll call in every day if that keeps you steady."

A laugh, half-breath and half exhale. "Don't threaten me with accountability. I might actually hold you to that."

"Promise. I've got you. You're not alone in this."

The sun drifts across the guest room, tracing gold over crumpled sheets and a jacket slung across the chair—a remnant of last night's fatigue. Elara leans back, letting the quiet wrap around her, gathering whatever scraps of resolve remain.

The penthouse hushes under the afternoon's stretch, tension pooled in the corners where arguments still echo. Orion sits finally, alone, dusk sliding its shadow over the study. He traces the blurred edge of a photograph: his sister's smile, Nova's small hands clutching tight to family that now feels perilous and fragile. In the next room, Elara locks her phone, her jaw set, ready to step back into the storm if that's what it takes to keep Nova—and the man she's beginning to care for—from drifting any further away.

Late afternoon unfurls across the upper city in a sheet of volatile silver, the penthouse absorbing the gloom with a shiver. Orion Vega thumbs through the messages on his secure comm, his jaw tight. His reflection ripples in the glossy surface of the study window—nothing but a specter haunted by too many fights, too little sleep. Alerts from board members scrawl across the interface, but it's not those that snag his pulse.

A new file. Encryption layered heavily, sender unlisted, flagged urgent with a glyph not even his firewall recognizes. He taps, cold dread crawling up his arms as the file bypasses every filter. The screen stutters, then unfurls a single, chilling sentence in stark, unadorned type: Shadows lengthen around towers of glass—hold the child close, they are coming.

The air in the study pinches tight, faint cinnamon from an abandoned mug colliding with the metallic scent of electronics. Orion yanks his chair closer, fingers dancing over secondary security systems. He cross-references the device log, finds nothing—but the message radiates intent, as if the sender pressed a finger to his spine.

His hand trembles, just once, before he dials the emergency comm channel. Caius's face flickers to life, framed by polished mahogany and the faint suggestion of a boardroom cityscape.

"They got through the failsafe, Caius. Some ghost, Helios maybe. The message—listen." Orion reads the words aloud, his voice hoarse.

Caius listens in silence, his eyes narrowing, then: "Sit rep?"

"Nothing on the system. No breach, no trace. Just that sentence—like they dropped it here, in the middle of everything."

"Double the protocols," Caius says, his voice all predatory calm. "Snoopers got closer than we thought. If they're inside our walls, they're watching. Log everything, no matter how small. This looks coordinated, Orion."

"Coordinated how?"

"We had similar attempts at two satellite offices this morning. PR is already spinning—rumors, dirty leaks, paparazzi with new lenses. Someone's sharpening knives, and they're not working alone. This is a squeeze, not just against you, but the Brotherhood as a whole."

"Copy that. I'll lock it down. Do not let the board get wind of this."

Caius's response is clipped. "Already on it. And Orion—watch your shadows. The city isn't what it was."

The line drops. Orion hovers over the blank screen. For a moment, he considers the whiskey in the study's shadows, but the thought dissolves—he needs to be sharper now than ever.

The penthouse is hushed, every surface more reflective as the sun dips, diffusing light through glass and steel. Orion's thoughts snag on jagged memories: Not long ago, he'd have solved a crisis like this by detonating a distraction and running—fast, loud, reckless, leaving others to sweep up the fallout. But Nova's face hovers near the surface of his mind, fragile as blown glass. Elara's steady voice—acerbic, fierce, unyielding—follows, both chain and anchor.

Out in the hallway, Elara's footsteps fade against polished marble. She pauses by a bank of windows, her hair backlit amber by the waning light. Two black vehicles idle on the curb, unmarked and inert, their sides capturing fractured images of the city. A man leans near the building's rear access, camera raised beneath his hood. When her eyes meet his, the stranger shifts, the shutter's click invisible but deafening in the hush.

Elara's breath hitches. She slips back into the shadows, pulse flaring, mind mapping exits and fallback points. The world outside has shifted—money, security, pedigree, none of it enough to mend the cracks threading through their safehouse.

In another wing, Nova crouches over her sketchbook. Colored pencils, waxy and warm, shudder on the page as she draws the city skyline. A shadow—long, mean—crosses her window, and Nova freezes. Her hands flutter, delicate as moths. Gently, she closes the curtains, double-checking the notched lock before crawling onto her bed.

Orion moves to the east windows, the city yawning before him, every office spark a potential watcher's lens. He leans against the glass, breath fogging a transient mark. His own penthouse—once an untouchable high-rise fortress—feels suddenly too open, its seams exposed. The world below seethes: corrupt boardrooms, syndicates, propaganda, all vying to expose and devour any weakness. Old power structures are unspooling. Even within walls thick with technology, the old rules no longer protect.

Responsibility settles over Orion's shoulders like a sodden cloak. He knows now: every misstep, every wound in the household, is a crack for their enemies to exploit. Years of running, of hiding behind bravado, have left him unprepared for this siege. The tension between his old self—impulsive, clever, untouchable—and the guardian Elara demands gnaws at him. He's afraid, in ways he hasn't admitted, that he can't outthink or outrun what comes next.

Elara stands quietly in the corridor, pressing her fingers to the window's edge, counting heartbeats, inventorying each threat she can't quite see. Nova's door is closed. Their breakfast quarrel still echoes in the silence.

Orion doesn't move as the city lights blink on, one by one, a constellation both beautiful and menacing. He keeps vigil long after dusk, aware that what stalks them comes closer with every flickering shadow—until the fortress around his family feels as thin and perilous as glass.

Domestic Storms

Warm lamplight pools over the pale blue walls of Nova's room, catching on paper stars taped to the ceiling and the rainbow of books stacked on the shelves. The smell of lavender lingers, subtle but calming, filling the space beneath the gentle hum of the air conditioning and the soft rustle of sheets. Elara settles onto the edge of Nova's little bed, her weight dipping the mattress just enough to reassure. One hand holds out Nova's beloved sloth—worn in places, more gray than brown—while the other angles a picture book toward the child. Nova's dark coils spill over the pillow, her eyes wide, fingers plucking absently at the tasseled edge of her blanket.

Elara glances at the stand: a water glass aligned so it won't spill, a nightlight already casting golden circles across the sheet, the blanket drawn up but not too tightly. All her movements are measured and unhurried, the practiced choreography of evening routines. She cracks the spine of the book and begins to read. Her voice is low and slow, each word deliberate as the story meanders through the adventures of a moonlit fox. The images flicker on the page in washes of indigo and silver, painting the quiet hush that fills the room.

The door opens with a faint soft click. Orion appears—shoulders squared, a dark blur in the half-light, holding a glass of water so over-sized that it sloshes dangerously close to the rim. He nearly loses his balance on the thick carpet and mutters something under his breath, his cheeks coloring as he sets the glass down beside Nova's smaller cup. His eyes flick to the book in Elara's lap. For a moment, he's the strange note in this familiar song—too big, too restless, all angular movements and nervous glances.

He clears his throat and edges closer to the bed. He studies the blanket, then Nova's bare feet, then back to Elara as if awaiting instruction on a protocol he's never learned.

"Uh... should I help with—" He nods toward the blanket, hesitating.

Elara cocks an eyebrow, shifting so he can reach. With gentle direction, she takes his fumbling hands and guides them, steadying his grip while he smooths the blanket over Nova's legs. His hands are awkward but careful, fingers lingering as if surprised by the quiet weightlessness of such a simple task.

Nova forms a small hill beneath the covers, her breaths slow and softening, watching the adults with a sidelong glance. Elara gives her shoulder a reassuring squeeze, her voice barely above a whisper. "You're safe, sweetheart. Nothing's going to get you while I'm here. I promise."

There's a flutter in Nova's chest, like tiny moth wings trapped inside. But something about this ritual—the book's gentle rise and fall, Elara's steady scent of rose and tea, the blanket wrapped just so—anchors her. Her hands, once balled into nervous fists, uncurl; her shoulders relax and settle against the cool cotton of her pillow.

"I like when you read," Nova murmurs, her words muffled by the sloth's scruffy fur. The smile that creases her face is fragile but real, blooming in the space between one breath and the next. The squeeze of fear in her stomach starts to loosen, replaced by the soft warmth of trust, the hope—however quiet—that tonight the monsters will stay outside her room.

Elara finishes the story, closing the book without a flourish. She shifts so she can place the volume back on the shelf, nodding a silent goodnight to the cast of illustrated animals. Nova's eyelids are already drooping, her lashes trembling as she blinks at the ceiling, where lamplight makes stars out of ordinary tape.

She looks over Nova's head, where Orion stands, hands shoved into his pockets, watching with a guarded intensity. His usual smirk is missing; in its place is a gravity she hasn't seen in him before, a silent question: Am I doing any of this right?

Elara meets his gaze. The wary antagonism that once colored every look between them is softer now—a truce struck, at least for this hour. She inclines her head, not quite a smile, more an acknowledgment. Orion, instead of deflecting or bristling, gives a quiet nod back. It is awkward but sincere—a gesture of thanks layered awkwardly over apology.

Elara brushes a stray curl from Nova's brow and tucks the sloth beneath her chin. The hush stretches, filled only by the tick of the clock and the city's far-off drone. After a moment, Nova, all but gone to sleep, draws the sloth close and lets her eyes close completely. Her breathing is even, her body slack in the safe cocoon they've built from repetition and gentle words.

Both Elara and Orion linger. She waits for his next ill-timed joke, the disruption that never comes. He holds the space in silence, uncertainty baring his edges but staying quiet. They look at Nova—small, fragile, but peaceful now. Their eyes meet above her, reluctance giving way to the first hint of shared purpose.

The adults slip from the room on silent feet, the hush behind them undisturbed. In the hallway, neither says a word. Tension drifts between them, but it's softer now, an undercurrent rather than a barrier—a guarded, necessary collaboration forged in the dim glow of a child's bedtime.

The penthouse kitchen always looks like it's been summoned from another world: chrome, glass, and light so precise that it casts everything in high relief. But tonight, the counters are pocked with flour, eggshells, and chaos—ripe for disaster, alive with possibility.

Orion strides in, tossing the eggs from palm to palm as if they're tech prototypes and not fragile, ovoid worlds. His announcement echoes against the steel—"Stand back, I'm in the mood for a masterpiece"—but his hands move too quickly, cracking eggs straight onto the marble counter and sending yolks skittering across the surface. The carton bounces, lands sideways, and drops its last soldier onto the floor with a soft thud. Across the island, Elara's brow arches. She's already clutching a whisk, her eyes wary but her lips pressed together, as if she refuses to let the night's hard-won peace be shattered by culinary hubris.

"You could—maybe just lay everything out first," she says, her voice low but edged with hope—or maybe exasperation. She moves with the clean authority of someone used to children and accidents, not chaos made by a man who revels in disorder.

Orion barely glances up. "Prep is for the scared and the sluggish." He dumps a fistful of flour onto the induction cooktop, then realizes his mistake as a cloud puffs out, settling over his dark forearms and catching blue LED light like space dust. He grins, half-defiant, half-mischievous. There's a smell of scorched flour and something deeper—his restlessness, his need to fill the silence left in the wake of order.

Eggshells stick to the side of a clear glass bowl. Still, Elara takes a measured breath, adjusting her stance as if bracing for impact, and begins issuing instructions with the gentle firmness of command. "Not all at once. That's a triple recipe's worth of cheese, Orion—"

He's already dumped a mound of white cheddar into the pan, where it hisses and pops, cascading down the side and beginning its slow death on the burner. "Scientific innovation means improvisation. You should try it sometime." There's a wink in his voice, even if his hands look almost deliberate in their disregard for caution.

Elara's eyes narrow, but her lips twitch. He can see it—her mask threatening to slip. She lifts her hand to rub her temple but catches herself. She almost laughs. The whisk stands idle.

There's a sudden squeak of footsteps just outside the threshold. Nova appears, peeking around the corner, her hair tangled from bedtime and her eyes still soft from story worlds. She stops, takes in the scene—a flour-splattered billionaire, a skeptical tutor, and a kitchen that smells of burnt toast and charred ambition. As Orion tries—disastrously—to flip a pancake with a flick of his wrist, the blob launches skyward, turns, then lands with a splat across the chest of his shirt.

A beat. Elara's control fractures irreparably. She tips her head back with a short, warm laugh—quick and sharp as breaking glass but threaded with relief. Nova claps her hand over her mouth, then loses all composure, laughter tumbling out in bright, spiraling notes. The kitchen, so often a gallery of silence and surface, rings with their joy.

Orion stares at the wet circle blooming across his shirt, momentarily incredulous, then shrugs and wipes at the mess with a kitchen towel far too clean for the task. Smears of batter mark him as a participant, not an overlord. He looks at Elara, his eyes gleaming.

"Now, you see," he says, holding up the unfortunate specimen, "this is what peak innovation looks like. You won't find this on any cooking show. Call it—chaos cuisine."

Elara, still catching her breath, adopts a mock-serious tone. "Genius, I'm sure. But next time, maybe wait until the pan's actually hot?"

Nova's giggles renew at this, and Orion, somewhat emboldened, flourishes the spatula like a baton. "Next time, I'll build the pan myself. The world's not ready for what I can do with a soldering iron and a cheese grater."

"That's what I'm afraid of," Elara says, but her voice holds none of the barbed tension from days before. The banter bounces between them, the old friction softened to something bright-edged and teasing, an alloy stronger than resistance.

For a long moment, the three of them only listen to the kitchen's new sounds: the sizzle and pop, the snap of crust breaking as Orion pries an omelet—scorched and misshapen—from the skillet. Nova's laughter lingers deep in the space, turning sterile air homely and inviting. Orion glances at her, and Elara follows his gaze—measured, tentative. In Nova's smile, there is something they both recognize: an opening, a possibility. A child's belief in togetherness, undampened by history.

Orion plates a heap of eggs, burnt edges curling like scrolls, and slides it in front of Nova with a flourish. "For you, m'lady. Dinner—improvised by disaster."

Nova solemnly picks up her fork, her eyes wide with mischief. "It's delicious." Then she laughs, and the adults follow, the sound rising, overlapping, cresting over a memory of what family could feel like: something messy, loud, alive. For a rare, crystalline moment, the penthouse hums with warmth, a shared gravity drawing them all closer.

Nova's drawings are everywhere—spilling across the gleaming marble floor in a kind of quiet rebellion against the penthouse's order. Elara steps through the scattered clouds of crayon and pastel, her bare feet making no sound. She crouches beside a half-finished page, the pinks and violets messy and bright beneath the LED glow. Her voice is low and coaxing, nothing of the strict schoolmistress but rather a gentle thread weaving through the static hush of evening. "You've nearly finished this nebula, Nova. Do you want to show me how you'll draw the stars?"

A tentative nod from Nova, and Elara's hand hovers, not to correct or force, just to encourage. There's strength in the way she waits, patient amid the city-lights haze, not pushing too hard. Orion lingers on the sofa's edge, a laptop balanced on his knees, fingers curled stiff and aimless over the keys. He watches, not quite hidden, not quite willing to insert himself. The sight of Elara kneeling at Nova's side, the curve of her back as she leans close, pulls at something buried inside him—a realization that real leadership, real guardianship, isn't a matter of declaration but of these small, deliberate acts.

Elara gathers stray markers, stacking them with efficient precision, and glances Orion's way. He can see how she checks on Nova without smothering, how she knows exactly when to step back. When Nova, shoulders tight and jaw set, presses a scrap of paper into Elara's hand, Elara accepts it without question. Orion registers the softness in her face, and for just a heartbeat, jealousy hums—he wishes he could make Nova uncurl like that, so simply, so surely.

He stands, stretches, and sets his laptop aside. The hush of the city feels more present in the penthouse tonight. No pounding music, no screens flickering bright. Instead, there's the hush of the filtration vents and the heavy dusk pressing against the glass.

As Nova migrates toward the wide cream sofa, Elara swoops up the discarded pillows, fluttering them back into their places. The angle of her shoulders is relaxed now, a touch of ease settling in. Orion notices because he's unaccustomed to the sensation himself—a room without tension, a night without carefully policed boundaries.

He takes a woolen throw, and as Nova curls inward on the cushions, he spreads it over her small form. For once, his large hands seem to move without awkwardness. He tucks the edge beneath Nova's chin—she barely stirs, but her fingers clutch the fabric as though it might anchor her to some secret safe place. Elara's gaze meets his, and an unspoken breath passes between them: a moment of mutual recognition, not of triumph or defeat, but of some subtle grace neither quite knows how to own.

A smile tugs at Elara's lips—a real one, quick as a meteor—and she catches herself before it breaks fully loose. She wasn't expecting gentleness from him, not after the headlines, not after the bluster. Orion feels heat prickle across the back of his neck. He returns to his armchair, letting the leather creak beneath his weight, and folds his arms as if to protect the strange new quiet.

Nova stares between the two of them, her gaze clouded and vulnerable, then drifts over, climbing silently into Elara's side. Small arms encircle Elara's waist. Nova burrows close, her voice a hush: "I like it when we're all here. I feel... safe." She blinks against Elara's shirt, her eyelids heavy. Elara holds her, and for a moment, Orion would trade every flashbulb moment in his gaudy public life for the simple solidity of this—Nova's dark curls pressed against Elara, the slow rise and fall of their breathing syncing up.

He's always thought of home as a fortress, a shield against outside disaster, all hard edges and locked doors. But this hush, filled with nothing but shared breath and the distant hum of city life, makes him wonder if he's been wrong all along. He studies the two of them—Elara's hand splayed at Nova's back, Nova's sleepy smile, the hush that gentles his own pulse.

"Night, Nova," Elara whispers, smoothing the hair from Nova's brow.

Orion lets the words fill him. He doesn't interrupt.

He leans his head back. For once, he's not calculating, not searching for the next threat. There's just the city's pulse twinkling through the glass, the soft exhale as Nova drifts toward sleep, Elara's profile etched in shadows and low light.

"You're good at this," Orion says finally, his voice low.

Elara glances over. "At what? Wrangling chaos or bedtime hugs?"

"Both."

She huffs a laugh, soft, and the tension leeches from her shoulders.

For a while, the three of them are simply present. No one talks. Nothing needs to be decided, defended, or denied. Orion's mind quiets—fear doesn't let go, not fully, but hope floats in the silent space between them.

Nova shifts, tucked into Elara's arms, and sighs—the sound as unguarded as anything Orion's ever known. He traces the arc of their gentle bond, feeling the storm inside him slow.

All the scars and jagged corners don't matter, not tonight. With Elara beside Nova, with the weight of trust forming in the hush, Orion finds himself wishing—not for escape, not for conquest, but for another night like this. For the first time in years, he believes it might be possible.

The three remain, bound in silence as the city's neon glow whispers over them, until the room feels less like a penthouse and more like the fragile beginning of home.

Attraction Ignites

A sudden darkness stamps out the penthouse—gone are the city's constellations of electric light, the skyline swallowed by a velvet curtain of storm, rain smearing the windows in racing rivers. The hum of hidden machines dies. For an instant, only the wild heartbeats of thunder, the brittle staccato of wind against glass, and the scent of ozone remain.

Elara's voice slices through the silence. "Stay still. Don't move until your eyes catch up." A flicker of movement—the beam of a phone screen thrown awkwardly toward the floor, blue-white and uncertain, glancing off cold marble.

Orion straightens, restless in the hush, his shape outlined only by the restless city beyond—now a smudge of gray, punctuated by distant neon bleeding through the rain. "Relax," he says, his voice pitched low with a brittle edge, "I know this place better blind than most people do with a map." But she's already moving, confident and ordered, one hand trailing the island to orient herself.

They collide in the narrow passage, shoulder to shoulder—her deliberate, his hurried. The brush of fabric, a fleeting jolt, a muttered, "Watch it," from Orion, mirrored by a crisp, "Maybe don't leave chairs pulled out like tripwires."

Elara's fingers find the drawer, sliding it open with methodical clicks. The metal inside clatters—batteries, a muddle of takeout menus, a tangle of odds and ends. "You call this organized?" She's all exposed patience; the sound of her sorting is brisk, surgical.

Thunder claws at the sky, each rumble vibrating the cutlery in the drawer and rattling the cabinets. Orion grins, unworried by the chaos. "Who needs order when you can improvise?" Yet there's something forced, half-mocking in his tone.

A second stumble—he reaches in, knocking over the canisters. Elara gives him a look that could break stone, the candle in her grip raised accusingly. "If Nova needs to get to her inhaler and everything's piled in the back, is improvisation your strategy then?"

The air is charged in ways the storm can only imitate. He means to snap back, but she cuts him off. "Go find matches. Not a lighter. Matches." She's already ticking off obstacles—locks the terrace doors with a decisive click, drapes a kitchen towel over the wet windowsill, and lines up candles beside the stovetop in military array.

Orion stalks off with a theatrical sigh, but silence reveals the restlessness beneath. He shuffles through the pantry, breath shallow. Disarray is something he swears by—every childhood memory stained by adults demanding order, imposing routines that made him itch beneath his skin. Elara, in this half-light, is the ghost of every rule he's learned to break. And yet there's a steadiness in her—her methodical hands, her unfussed pace, the certainty in her commands. It stings, but he feels almost drawn.

The glow of his phone dwindles as he sifts through the second drawer. The scent of dust and faint vanilla—some box of cookies long gone—mixes with the chemical bite of the storm. He finally locates the matches, flipping them in his palm, letting the rattle fill the emptiness. He could let the night go feral, let the darkness swallow everything, but now he walks back, driven by her wordless expectation.

With each new candle lit, the kitchen carves itself back out of the dark: marble counters blushed by trembling gold, shadows pooling under the cabinets, glass gleaming like lake water at midnight. Elara remains in sharp focus now, her face a study of calm under stress, light painting her cheekbones, eyes intent on the wavering flames. Order spreads from her hands, infects the room—the world itself seems quieter, the storm a little further away.

Orion plants the matches on the counter, arms folded, his voice dry. "Sure you don't want to draw up a battle plan first?" He's half-jesting, half-defensive.

"I prefer not to trip over hubris in the dark," she replies, not glancing up. The tiniest smirk curves her lips before vanishing, but he catches it—a flicker of amusement and challenge.

They navigate the last of the preparations, steps overlapping but never quite aligning. The kitchen hums with the wariness of two commanders forced onto the same field, neither willing to yield but both aware of the other's strengths. Elara's authority is unshowy, self-contained—a far cry from the chaos Orion brandishes like armor. It needles him, but it also disarms him, leaving him wondering whether discipline is its own kind of blade.

A hush settles as Elara strikes the final match. Sulfur tangs the air, sharp and familiar. The last candle ignites, doubling the warm glow and throwing their shadows long, monstrous, and oddly intimate against the metal and glass. For a brief moment, the world shrinks to the ring of light between them.

Elara levels her gaze at him—steady, unbending, the unspoken warning that her order will not falter, storm or no storm. Across from her, Orion stands motionless, the candlelight catching in his eyes, revealing more than he's willing for her to see. The tension between them—push and pull, command and resistance, heat and uncertainty—flares in the darkness, unresolved, humming like a power line waiting for the city to remember its current.

Morning turns Orion's study into a battlefield—the kind that hums with artificial daylight instead of steel and gunpowder. The city's storm's retreat left behind a residue of rain slipping down the mammoth windows in slow, silvery rivers. Inside, order is a myth. Scattered papers form makeshift snowdrifts along the black marble floor, blueprints curling like the tails of restless beasts, coffee rings blooming on Nova's school reports. The scent is a blend of cold metal, old paper, and the ghost of last night's rain dampening the velvet runner atop his desk. Three empty energy drink cans stack in a pyramid of shame beside the smudged screen of Orion's tablet.

Elara's footsteps, composed and unhurried, slip into the mess with the silent inevitability of a tide overtaking a sandcastle. She stands in the doorway, arms crossed over a pale blue sweater, her presence a pinpoint of steadiness in a space designed for improvisation and upheaval. Her gaze coasts methodically across the wreckage—papers splayed, cans tipped, one of Nova's glitter pens teetering on a precarious stack of technical drawings.

"Is this how you want her to study?" Elara's tone slices through the air thick with electrons and unspoken argument. "Chaos on every surface, nothing where it belongs. You want Nova to feel steady here? She barely sets down her bag without tripping over last night's 'insp iration.'"

Orion stands at the window with his back tense, one arm braced upon the glass as if holding up the night itself. He whirls—a quick, kinetic movement, eyes sparking with something between challenge and fatigue.

"Organization by your standards means everything would be dead. Processed. I do my best work here—" He gestures to the debris, the blueprints, the tangles of wire peeking from beneath a half-assembled drone. "Some of us create lightning out of the storm, Elara." Defensive ire rises in each syllable.

"Lightning burns down houses, too," she says quietly. Her eyes never flinch.

A beat stretches between them, filled by the gentle percussion of rain, the slow drip from a leaking gutter somewhere out of sight.

"This isn't about you," Elara insists, her voice pitched low yet unwavering. "It's about Nova—her hands shake every time she does her homework here. All this clutter, all your... momentum—it isn't just yours anymore. She feels it." Her arms are still folded, her expression steady. "She deserves peace, Orion. Not another storm in every room."

For a moment, he wants to spit back—rebuke, sarcasm, barbed deflection. Instead, guilt slinks in, unwelcome but too familiar. Last night flashes behind his eyes: Nova's wide stare in the candlelight, her breath starting to spiral before Elara calmly pressed a hand to her back and spun disaster back into quiet. Under the surface, something fragile flexes in him.

He looks away, jaw working a rhythm of denial and unease. "I'm doing what I can to keep us whole. My way doesn't fit your charts or your lesson plans, but it's what I know."

Elara moves past him, collecting papers, stacking books. Each gesture is deliberate, a metronome marking the measure of stability he pretends to despise. She checks the pile of Nova's worksheets, smoothing a spilled cup off a folder. "You don't have to like it," she says, almost gently, "but you're not the only one who lives here anymore. If you want her to feel safe, this needs to change. Not for me. For her."

He says nothing, letting the words hit him and scatter.

She exits swiftly, footsteps crisp against the stones. In her wake, she pauses outside the door, then turns and begins straightening the shelf outside the study—a stack of biographies, a dusty photo of Orion's sister, the edges square and even under her steady hands.

The silence left behind hums—a presence all its own. Orion remains frozen in the cluttered center, pulse drumming in his throat. He should be furious. This was always his world: kinetic, shifting, too expansive for rules and checklists. But the argument's echo claws through him, dragging up a hollow ache. How many times did he promise Nova he'd protect her from chaos—then flood her with his own?

Shame prickles under his skin, yet defiance simmers stubbornly. He is a storm, not a gentle rain. Structure might keep the world from slipping out of control, but what if that same structure strangles the part of him that builds, dreams, survives? His mind spirals: what would it be to let someone else's order in, to trust those calm hands instead of always bulldozing his own path forward?

He watches Elara at the shelf: the sure, quiet strength of her, the relentless way she rights what's toppled—never just scolding but restoring. There's something magnetic there, a steadiness that unsettles as much as it soothes. Orion wonders what it would be to let that steadiness root itself in the core of this home, to let her certainty spill into the cracks he's spent years prying open. What would he become—worse, what would he lose—if he surrendered even a corner of his chaos for her brand of peace?

Rain beats out a thin rhythm on the glass. The city beyond his window appears sharp and endless, but here in the study, the world narrows to candle wax remnants and the faint, lingering trace of vanilla from Elara's perfume.

He lingers in the doorway, silent, watching her restore order—one careful gesture at a time—as the room hushes and the only thing left moving is the rain.

The air on the balcony carries the last chill of rainfall, sharp with the scent of ozone and wet concrete. Water beads on the tempered glass railing, illuminated by shafts of sunlight that break through battered clouds and scatter prisms across the marble. Below, the city's pulse has slowed, as if even the engines and voices out there have paused to catch their breath. At this height, the storm's memory still lingers—a low grumble on the horizon, the world slick and raw and washed clean.

Elara stands with her back against the sleek door for a moment, letting the noise from the penthouse fall away. Her hands press into the cool surface behind her, anchoring her in this rare chance at quiet. Orion is already there, arms braced wide on the glass, his shadow long against the polished floor. His shirt is wrinkled from a day's worth of tension; the cuff escapes his sleeve, showing a flash of the faded scar he usually keeps hidden. He doesn't turn. He watches the fractured skyline, eyes narrowed as if reading a secret language written in sun and storm clouds.

Rain-washed air presses in, heavy and alive, prickling over Elara's skin. She moves to the edge, her steps soft against the marble, shoes forgotten somewhere inside. She stops a deliberate few feet away, balancing the space between proximity and caution.

"Strange how peaceful it looks after it's wrecked everything," she says quietly, fixing her gaze on the rippling gold reflected on steel towers. Her voice threads between them, gentle and measured, firm against the breeze.

Orion scoffs, a low sound. "It's a lie. Under all this calm, the grid's still fried and the board is probably in meltdown. Someone will call it an act of God while I hunt for the next fire to put out."

She glances sideways—a flicker, not a challenge. "You survived the actual storm, at least. The blackout. The kitchen chaos. And Nova's first panic since I got here." Her arms cross over her chest, fingers gripping her elbows. "Not everything fell apart."

Thunder stirs again, distant but insistent. Orion weighs her words. For once, she sees him hesitate—mouth pressed into a hard line, jaw tight, as if he's replaying that night in the candle-lit kitchen: her voice unwavering as she restored order, his resistance crumbling in small, undeniable ways. The city lights are just beginning to spark alive again. He blinks, slow and tired, then releases a held breath.

"She trusts you, you know," he says, his voice rough around the edges. "Nova used to avoid everyone. Now she dashes into the hallways again. Asks for your soup. Draws you as 'Miss Kent, Warrior of Math.'" His mouth twitches. "You're the only one who can get her to finish a meal lately."

A wick of warmth flares in Elara's chest, swift as a match struck in darkness. She schools her features, not letting it show. "Children need patterns. Structure. Someone has to be the anchor when everything else is moving."

He shifts, turning half toward her. The last sunlight catches in his eyes—deep and unreadable, the kind of gaze that makes her pulse quicken with both frustration and something almost like anticipation.

"Someone," he repeats, quiet now, as if the word is heavier than glass. "I wasn't looking for an anchor when I hired you. Didn't even want you here. But this place... there's less chaos. I find myself checking if you've shut the windows. Wondering if you've left a note. Some days, it's like breathing easier with you around."

A silence gathers, full and taut, stretching only as far as the sound of distant traffic and the hum of servers rising again inside. Elara feels it coil low in her stomach—a dangerous comfort. The urge to take responsibility for his peace flickers against the memory of every time she's bent too far, lost herself in fixing someone else's storm.

Her lips curve, subtle and wry, but her eyes are steady. "Stability's not surrender, Orion. Don't confuse my boundaries for permission to bulldoze through them. Anchor or not, I'm not here to be swept under by the tide."

He exhales, some knot in his body loosening. "Wouldn't dream of it." His hand runs through tousled hair, then falls to his side. "But you're braver than everyone in this building combined, coming in here and staking your claim on order. Even when I gave you every reason to run."

She smiles—fleeting, mysterious. "I haven't run yet." Sunlight breaks full across her face, catching in the lines of determination etched at her brow and the softness that keeps slipping in around Orion, despite every wall she raises.

He looks at her, something arrestingly serious in his expression. The storm has spent itself, but its energy lingers, a tension spun between the two of them as bright as the city crawling slowly back to life. Promise and friction fill the quiet, unspoken but thick in the air.

The sun slips out, painting the world gold, and for a moment, neither of them looks away.

The living room, washed in the lavender hush of early evening, feels changed by the storm's aftermath. The skyline is a fractured geometry of light—amber traffic weaving lower down, flickering orbs of emergency power pulsing from other towers, but up here the world feels suspended. Glass walls are painted with drifting, watery shadows. Orion and Elara stand near the long, low table, two figures locked in almost-wordless tension. Elara holds a plain envelope with Nova's school report inside; Orion glances at the neat columns and corrected spelling tests like he's deciphering a code left in an extinct language.

Outside, the city breathes in the silence that always follows a storm's passing, light bending against the wet glass, a neon afterglow staining Orion's profile as he looks at Elara. There's a question in the air—what now?—neither of them quite willing to say it. For a heartbeat, something softer catches between them, a near-vulnerability. Then a small, determined fist knocks the moment aside.

Nova bursts in, all wild hair and flushed cheeks, brandishing her homework sheet. She clutches it to her chest as if it's a talisman warding off disaster. "I... I need help! Mrs. Cardoza made this one really hard." She holds up the page; graphite numbers blur at the edge where her thumb smudged them.

Orion's posture shifts, armor sliding into place but softer this time. Elara's expression melts from wary calculation to one of practiced reassurance. Nova moves inexorably between them, gravity in miniature, pulling adults back down to her sphere.

Orion kneels, shoes squeaking softly against polished stone. "What'd she throw at you this time? Quantum calculus, or just regular math mean enough to ruin your day?" He tries for levity; the words stumble but earn a hesitant smile from Nova.

Elara lowers herself beside Nova, smoothing stray curls away from Nova's forehead with gentle fingers. "Let's see what the villainous worksheet has for us," she says, tone teasing but warm. She leans in, the faint scent of mint trailing from her—calm against the ozone that still lingers in the penthouse.

Orion pulls a pencil from behind Nova's ear—a trick, deft and unexpected. "Okay, scientist, lead us through the riddle." He hands it to her, fingers grazing hers, and throws a look to Elara. Not a wink, not a plea—something quieter. A silent thanks for holding the line when he couldn't earlier.

Nova explains the problem, her voice thin at first, then steadier as she describes numbers and the way they won't behave no matter how much she tries to wrangle them. Orion listens, nodding, asking questions that gently prompt but never crowd. Elara watches Orion with a flicker of humor at the way he makes a fraction sound like a puzzle box and not a threat.

Nova solves the first step. Orion grins. "See? You cracked the code. That's more than your old uncle did on most Mondays." Elara gives Nova a conspiratorial nudge, her own smile restrained but genuine as Nova's confidence blooms the barest bit. For a fragile moment, the room belongs only to them.

Elara hands over a clean eraser, nudging Nova's hand to fix a shaky symbol. "Even teachers mess these up. The trick is not letting the numbers see you sweat." Orion shakes his head—half at himself, half as if conceding to Elara's method—but his glance at her is not an argument, just recognition that the world can be rebuilt, one tiny mistake erased at a time.

Above, the city's pulse throbs through the glass, but in here, the only sound is the quiet scratch of graphite, the soft rhythm of Nova's breathing as her shoulders relax, the shared focus pulling them into a new orbit.

Their fingers nearly brush as they both lean in to look at Nova's answer. Orion and Elara share a glance—brief, reluctant, yet not without its own relief. An alliance, unspoken and perhaps only for tonight, forged in the small certainty of a solved equation and a child's shifting sense of safety.

Nova slides to the carpet, knees tucked under her skirt, her world narrowed to the worksheet poised on the low table between them. Orion settles beside her, one arm draped behind Nova but never quite touching—a shield, invisible but present. Elara sinks cross-legged across from them, her presence a steady metronome of calm.

Rain traces ghostly veins across the windows, but none of them move to close the curtains. The city beyond rages, rumors and boardroom warfare and shadowed conspiracies clicking into place. But inside, the storm breaks differently: in the hush of pencils, in Elara's balanced voice, in Orion's wary gentleness. For a breath, they are simply three people joined by the solving of a single, stubborn problem.

Orion watches Nova, his own heartbeat echoing the steady logic of numbers. This—this is the world he always feared he'd ruin. Yet here, with Elara anchoring one side and Nova trusting him to explain a line of math that once would've defeated his sister, he feels that maybe chaos is only the other side of hope. Maybe these moments, as frail as candle flames, can last long enough to build something real.

He meets Elara's eye. She doesn't speak, but her look is steadfast. For now, order is held—by her, by himself, by the small, insistent presence of the child between them. Nova leans, scribbling, impatient to reach the next problem. And in the uneven, tremulous warmth of the penthouse living room, night settling around them, they sit—together, unresolved, cocooned by the fragile quiet that their day's storms, somehow, have given them.

The Storm Kiss

Orion stands at the glass entrance, backlit by the flicker of a restless city skyline. Lightning cuts jagged, blinding veins through the clouds, spilling white patterns across the marble beneath his boots. His thumb swipes across the phone screen, half-watching, half-calculating his ruin, while thunder creeps across bone and glass. Outside, the wind hurls rain that drums on the window with the steady, merciless rhythm of protest. The penthouse is alive with the storm: steel and light, turbulence painted by nature and the mess he's made.

The hush inside is brittle, ready to crack. Footsteps, light but certain, rise from the velvet shadow of the library nook—Elara emerging, never quite on edge, but never wholly at ease here either. Lightning grazes her face as she takes in the scene: Orion, pacing, shoulders tense as drawn wire. Something electric hums between them, not just the gathering ozone, but the charge born of days spent circling one another, sparring for control, for some half-buried right to decide what makes a family.

He turns before she can speak, frustration flaring behind his eyes.

"Have you seen Nova?" Orion's voice stings—a low thrum, fraying with worry he's too proud to let show. "She was supposed to be here. Ten minutes ago."

Elara's gaze sharpens. "Maybe if you'd stuck to the routine she depends on, she wouldn't be hiding." Her words land like pebbles tossed into a pond—disruptive, quietly daring. "You promised you'd check in after her reading session. But you were busy—"

"I was dealing with another goddamn—" His jaw sets, muscles twitching. "Board email. I can't fight a custody war and hold your lesson plan hostage at the same time, Elara."

"And I can't fix Nova's panic if you keep making her guess when you'll actually show up," she says, her voice measured, even when she's shaking inside. "She needs a single thing she can count on. That's not too much for a child."

Rain slams harder, wind shuddering through the edges of the open balcony door. The wind seizes the glass, and for a heartbeat, the storm is in the room—icy water streaming across Orion's bare forearm, pelting through his shirtsleeve, licking down the marble in quicksilver channels.

Orion and Elara both lunge for the doors. Their hands meet at the threshold, rain drenching them in a shock of cold so sharp Elara gasps. Her hair, already wild from humidity, is plastered to her cheeks; Orion's shirt, tailored and pointless now, clings to him in heavy folds.

She tries to dart past him, shoving at the glass. Lightning explodes above, nearer this time, and in the white flash, her mouth opens on a warning that dissolves beneath the roar. Orion's hand closes around Elara's wrist—not rough, but inescapable, pulling her back into the tangle of water and heat.

Elara twists, lips parted, eyes blazing. "Let go," she hisses—a plea and a battle cry stitched together.

He does not. Instead, he draws her close, eyes locked on hers—dark, furious, longing blazing under the static-laced air between them.

"You overstep," Orion snarls, his voice roughened by too many nights of argument and guilt. "You come in and make rules like they mean more than anything else. I'm the one they'll rip apart in court. Not you."

She yanks her arm but doesn't break his grip. Water beads at her brow. "These rules are the difference between a home and another disaster, Orion. Nova needs boundaries—so do you, whether you admit it or not."

Thunder cracks. The sound rolls over them, drowning every rational retort. Orion's chest heaves; all his edges feel razor-bright—anger, fear, the desperate urge to keep everything from shattering. He lets go of her wrist only to cup her jaw, his thumb trembling against her pulse.

And just like that, he pulls her in—a kiss, fierce and raw, as rain slicks their skin and the wind howls around them. Orion's hands knot in Elara's soaked hair, desperate for an anchor. All the arguments, the insolent disregard, the resentment and the impossible wanting—they burn in that single, wild press of mouths.

Elara freezes. Her back stiffens, hands braced against his chest. In the space of a breath, the world outside—storm, doom, duty—vanishes. Her fingers knot in the fabric of his shirt, knuckles bloodless. She draws him closer, lips parting, letting herself be ruined by the gravity of this moment.

They break apart only when lightning fractures the dark again. Orion's breath is wild, each gasp tasting of rain and longing. His palm lingers at the edge of Elara's jaw; she leans in, forehead pressed to his, eyes shut as if she can hide from the reality of what they've just surrendered.

Now they stand entwined, trembling, rainwater pooling at their feet, the wildness inside the glass matching the wildness within. The city sprawls beneath, oblivious—a million lights, all distant and cold. In this small, soaked corner of Orion's empire, everything is uncertain except for the fire burning between them, set alight not despite their war, but because of it.

Orion stands, his shirt plastered to his skin, rivulets of rainwater running from his jaw down his throat, puddling on the marble floor. Elara's breath comes quick and fragile, shoulders pressed taut around her chest, arms entwined as if holding herself in place. Hair snakes over her cheeks, strands heavy with stormwater. Lightning flashes behind the glass, whitening the room for a heartbeat, outlining the stunned angles of Orion's face and the tangled shadow of Elara. Their kiss hovers in the charged air, its heat refusing to fade.

He tries to steady his breath, but his heartbeat slams into his ribs. It's as if the storm's electricity crawled beneath his skin and set everything trembling. He can taste her still—salt, heat, and thunder—and the echo of her lips seems louder than the pounding rain. Orion stares at her, not trusting his own hands. Not trusting his own hunger. The wall he's built between reason and feeling isn't just cracked—it's shattered, the shards glittering at his feet. What have I done? What did I let out? Fear prickles beneath the rush—fear of needing her, of exposing everything soft and breakable inside him, everything he spent years refusing to feel.

Elara doesn't meet his gaze. She draws herself tighter, as if she'd rather disappear than stand here dripping in front of him. Her skin glistens, goosebumps rising, lashes trembling, lips parted and tender.

The wildness between them is still here, still coiling through the room like vapor, but she's retreating behind composure, shoring up defenses even as her pulse—he can see it at the base of her throat—keeps racing. Her voice doesn't come. Orion aches to speak, to say anything sharp or flippant or real, but language has abandoned both of them.

Thunder rolls, rattling the glass with animal fury. The room gleams with reflections: lightning lashing blue across the marble, rain slanting in silver lines over the city below. This place was designed for control: lines clean and cold, order asserted over chaos. Yet here, now, Orion and Elara are wild and small and deeply human, shaking with something rawer than logic.

He inches forward, almost imperceptibly. One hand lifts—caught halfway between impulse and restraint—but he stops himself. What claim does he have? Desire is still burning in him, marking out all the places where control used to be. And underneath that: dread, so old it tastes like childhood. How many times has he pushed too far, demanded forgiveness he didn't earn? How many times did someone close their door on him, fed up with the storm he always brings?

She looks up. The lines of her face are fierce and uncertain, stubbornly real. He reads accusation, confusion, and a flicker of hope she's not ready to give voice to. How long have they been circling each other with swords drawn, pretending boundaries could save them? His own rules failed him long ago—Elara's, he's only just begun to understand. It's her boundaries that have made him crave order, crave not just this jolt of passion, but the gentler thing beneath: the trust of someone who won't let him blow their world open and walk away from the wreckage.

Minutes leak by, slow and sticky as honey. Neither moves. They cling to distance like it's the last life raft in a sea that wants to drown them.

"Elara—" His voice comes out raw, wrecked, too full.

She shakes her head, not ready. "Don't."

He drops his hand to his side, nails biting into his palm. Silence sprawls between them. The only sound is the rain, hissing against glass and licking at their ankles, the whole penthouse infused with ozone, panic, and guilty longing.

He remembers Nova—Nova's quiet struggles, the routines Elara built for her, the way Elara turned this place from battleground to home. Elara's rules, her stubborn refusal to be impressed or cowed by him—they've held everything together. Has he just fractured that, the one thing Nova clings to? He wants to apologize, and he wants to claim her, and neither action makes sense.

He almost asks her if she wishes it undone. He almost asks her if she's as terrified as he is.

Another rumble of thunder; the city glows molten and strange beyond the rain-soaked glass. Elara finally shifts her stance, still hugging herself, her gaze flitting past Orion's face like a moth desperate for darkness.

He doesn't know if moving toward her would make everything break, or if standing still will. For the first time in too long, Orion Vega is out of words and out of armor, left with nothing but the reverberant ache of what he wants and the sharp fear it might ruin them both.

He stands there, fists clenched, every muscle burning, while Elara lingers a breath away, eyes shadowed and shining. Thunder echoes past them, and only the rhythm of their breathing betrays how badly this moment has changed everything.

Nova crouches at the corner of the hallway, where dimming light from the windows halos the edge of the pale wall. Her small fingers leave nervous smudges on the paint, anchoring her as she peeks into the living room's hush. She sees Orion and Elara standing close, shields stripped down by the storm. Water drips steadily onto the marble, pooling around their shoes—black leather, sensible flats—evidence that, a minute ago, something had shocked the air still.

Orion's hand hovers in the charged silence. His gaze darts toward Elara, searching, maybe for anger, maybe for forgiveness. The lines of his body are set tight, yet his fingertips drift closer, longing to bridge the inches between them. Nova sees his chest rise and fall, harder and faster, as if he's run a great distance without moving from that spot. Elara's shoulders square defensively, lips parted, breath just audible above the rain. Then Orion's hand, as if with a will of its own, moves to Elara's—his thumb barely brushing her skin. Not a bold grip, but a gentle, uncertain tangle, palm-to-palm, like he's touching something breakable. Nova's held breath catches at the sight; she has never watched adults reach for each other with such careful slowness.

Thunder burrows into the glass, blunt and low, but in the room, everything sounds softer—softer than the hard-edged words she remembers slicing through dinnertime in an old house now quiet forever. The adults say nothing. Nova tries to count the shallow breaths that mix with the rain-muffled city below. It's a ritual in her secret mind: counting, because when numbers march in order, maybe the world will do the same. Fingers flex against the wall, grounding her. Tonight the storm outside seems far away, muffled by the cocoon of their nearness.

She presses herself further into the hallway's shade, half-shadow and half-eager. Rain-shimmer wobbles across the ceiling, refracted by tears on Orion's face or maybe just by the wetness from the storm. The apartment suddenly feels warmer to her, the kind of warmth that's not from heaters or sunlight, but from something that can fill up all the lonely spaces between people. She's seen cold silences—icy, bristling, the kind where someone stops talking and never starts again, where the rattle of plates means danger is coming, where tension tastes metallic on her tongue. Tonight's quiet is different. There's a twitch of hope nestled in it, as light as the scent of ozone curling inside the penthouse from the open balcony.

Bit by bit, Nova's heart—always balled up tight like a fist inside her chest—loosens. The spike of worry she carries, that one wrong word will shatter today as it's shattered so many yesterdays, ebbs just a little. She pictures Orion's hand resting in Elara's. That's not how angry people stand. That's not what people do when they're about to leave. Images flutter in her mind: her mother and Orion, long ago, laughing over burnt cookies; days before storms and funerals and new rules. It's always been safest to stay out of sight, to keep her head down, to shrink herself down small so she wouldn't get caught in the riptide of someone else's hurt. But tonight, the world feels slightly braver.

She stands straighter, watching Elara's lips move.

"Nova's asleep," Elara whispers.

Orion whispers back, "She'd be terrified if she saw us like this."

"We should get changed." For a moment, Elara's voice sounds softer than Nova has ever heard it—tired, yes, but folded in a kind of gentle patience.

Orion's hand squeezes hers, the contact feather-light and trembling.

"Don't go," he says. "Not yet."

A hush follows. The only reply is the symphony of the city, rain and thunder and the faint pulse of traffic below.

Nova lets herself drift backward, hopeful. The bruised light from the windows fades, and as dusk steals across her toes, she pads to her room. Each step feels lighter, the awful tightness in her chest loosening into something almost fluttery—barely-there joy. She pictures invisible threads, spun by hands both strong and gentle, knotting together where they touch.

At her door, Nova glances back. Orion and Elara have not moved. They stand shadow-limned, joined now by something invisible, fragile. The room breathes possibility into the storm-washed air. Nova closes her door softly, mindful not to break the spell. Beyond, thunder smudges into silence, and hope, small but bright, finds root behind her ribs, daring that maybe this, too, could be a beginning.

Growing Passion and Vulnerability

Nova's breathing has settled into gentle, even waves behind the closed door. The penthouse hangs in its midnight hush. Orion's bare feet pad soundlessly across the marble, every muscle still keyed to tension even as he descends into the sanctum of the living room. Overhead, city lights refract in the windows, smearing streaks of electric blue across the cold glass. He glances at Elara; in the soft gloom, she is all sharpened edges and quiet defiance, arms folded, gaze shadowed but steady.

She doesn't move to leave—almost as if she anticipates what he hasn't yet decided to ask.

He lifts a hand, motioning toward the low-lit bar. "I thought—maybe you'd stay. Just for a drink."

Elara's mouth quirks, a wary acceptance. She perches at the edge of the sofa, her back straight as a blade, the hem of her sweater brushing the curve of white leather. Orion pours two fingers of whiskey, the bottle's neck yawning amber, and the liquid biting the air with oaken warmth. He brings her a glass without flourish and settles across from her. Space yawns between them—the black sculpted coffee table, the kind of chasm that feels geographical as well as emotional.

He rolls the glass between his palms, the surface catching blue-white city glimmers. Silence shivers between them, taut and expectant, uneven as their heartbeats.

"Elara." His voice is a hush, raw as stone and new as confession. "Do you ever just... not know what the hell you're doing? Like you're meant to protect something precious but you're all wrong for it. Like the universe got the addresses mixed up. And now—" He exhales, the sound scraping low in his throat. "Now I'm at the helm of a ship I never built, with a crew I never chose to lead."

She studies him—the mess of his hair, the unsettled set of his jaw. Her own fingers are tight around her glass, but she's still, as if she's marking a turning in weather she expected but couldn't prepare for.

"My sister." Orion's next words hover, tasting of burnt honey and regret. "She was the one who knew how to love. Effortlessly. Even when life chewed her up and spit her out, she anchored everyone. I was the storm, and she was the... the harbor. When she died, I thought, 'How am I supposed to raise her kid?'" His chest knots. "Nova deserves better. Sometimes I look at her and all I see is how close I am to screwing it up."

In the hanging pause, the city pulses like a distant heart. Elara sets her drink down, the faint clink breaking the tension's brittle skin. Her shoulders lower—not in defeat but in a careful lowering of armor.

"I know what instability does," she says, her voice soft but steady. "My parents divorced twice, if you count what came after the lawyers, the remarriages, the houses that were never home. I swore I'd build something different. But every time I let someone in, I end up bracing for the moment it all unravels. Patterns… they find you, even when you think you're too smart for them."

"Maybe everyone's winging it, huh?" Orion's lips twitch in the outline of a smile, but the shadow of old guilt dogs his words. "I keep thinking if I outsmart the world, I'll finally deserve her. Doesn't work, does it?"

Elara's brow furrows. "Deserving has nothing to do with it. It's just… staying. Even when you're scared out of your mind."

He wants to believe that. He wants to reach for the premise of worth written not in brilliance or wealth but in the small moments—staying when it's easier to run.

She leans forward, sleeves whispering along the table. Her hand lands over his, warm and dry; her thumb brushes that old scar on his arm, the one that's always marked him as reckless, too quick to risk.

They are a circuit now—current arcing painfully steady between touch and silence. His gaze drops to where their hands meet, and for a breath, the room recedes. All the machinery, glass, and blue-lit surfaces blur at the periphery.

Orion's thoughts churn—grief and gratitude, fear and longing, each emotion pricking raw against his nerves. He's spent years building walls of steel, hiding behind work, control, and clever retorts. But Elara—she lets the ache stand, accepts the truth without flinching. Their antagonism was always armor—a way to keep from splintering.

This is what it means to let go, he realizes. Not in grand gestures but in letting someone see the seams, the places you're certain will come apart under scrutiny. Her touch is unadorned, undemanding, patient.

The city outside is relentless, neon and infinite. But the living room holds like a capsule; the only real thing is this hush, electric and perilous and full of promise. His breath syncs with hers, slow and uncertain.

Their hands stay joined, not moving, as if movement would shatter the fragile trust blooming in their shared silence. The night hums—alive, unknown.

Morning lays gentle claim to the penthouse, sunlight pooling across the floor-to-ceiling window and slipping over the library nook's shelves, as if granting grace to a place seldom at peace. In Nova's study, the air carries the sharp scent of fresh paper, graphite, and something faintly sweet—lemon verbena from the pot in the window. Nova sits upright, her ponytail a shadow against the wash of daylight, brows knit over her exercise book. Her eraser hovers midair; Elara traces the curve of the girl's shoulder, the steady rise and fall of breath that no longer quivers with every new word.

"'Stratosphere,'" Nova says, careful but braver than yesterday.

Elara nods, suppressing the urge to praise with fanfare—Nova shies from too much light, as if words themselves can burn. Instead, she offers low, steady encouragement. "You've got it. Just a few more, then we'll let the crabs out for breakfast."

Nova's lips curve, the first emerging smile of the day, and her pencil scratches across the page with quiet confidence. Around them, the penthouse hums with a distant silence, a world apart from the cacophony Elara grew up in—one of doors slamming, arguments echoing like a stovetop kettle. Here, the loudest thing is the impossibility of what was whispered the night before.

Elara glances at the closed door as Nova turns to write her final answer. She remembers the living room: the low light gilding Orion's profile in gold, his hands wound tight around a tumbler, the false bravado leeched away as he'd said, I'm terrified I'll ruin her. Elara feels the ghost of that confession stirring under her breastbone; a weight, and strangely, a lightness, too. She hadn't expected someone like Orion to admit his terror, his fear at being left holding the pieces of a life torn by wind and scandal. It is difficult to reconcile that vulnerability with the man whose name headlines stock tickers and rumor sites like a storm warning.

Nova sighs, placing her pencil softly atop the notebook. "I'm done, Miss Kent." Her voice is stronger today, the vowels rounder; she glances up for approval, searching for something steadier than applause.

"You did wonderfully." Elara closes the exercise book with deliberate care, fingers resting on its spine as if committing something precious to memory. She wants to freeze the fleeting, sun-warmed moment, but Nova is already tiptoeing to the terrarium by the window, murmuring soft greetings to her tiny shelled companions.

Left in the quiet, Elara's composure cracks like sugar atop a brûlée. She lets her hands fall into her lap and stares at the shaft of gold illuminating the dust motes swirling in air gone hushed after confession. Her mind retraces last night, but memory slips from her grasp, trembling between hope and panic. She is not meant to be here like this: not as confidante, still less as something more. Her own childhood, rootless and unpredictable, whispers warnings in the back of her mind. She has spent so long constructing boundaries—careful routines, strict lines not to be crossed—yet last night, Orion's voice, rough and honest, summoned up the craving for something messier: the risk of belonging.

She watches Nova sprinkle food into the terrarium, the child's focus serene, utterly at home in the miniature world she tends. Elara wonders what would happen if she stayed, not out of contract or duty, but simply for this—the fragile mornings, the possibility of laughter that lives close behind sorrow. Orion's penthouse could become more than a post—could shelter the promise of partnership, if only she lets herself want it.

It seems foolish to long for a steady place beside a man who refuses stability even in sleep, who wears his wildness like armor. Still, a pulse of warmth climbs from Elara's stomach to her throat at the memory of his hand open—vulnerable—wondering aloud if he was failing Nova. She sees in him the battered hope of someone who wants desperately to do right, even if he doesn't know how. Would it be so bad, she muses, to give herself permission to dream—of dinners in the kitchen where laughter finally outpaces discord, of sharing morning coffees while the city stirs beneath them? She could imagine her voice tangled in his, the hard corners of caution softened by trust built, not demanded.

Yet doubt lingers, persistent. Love with Orion is chaos laced with lightning, a storm that could as easily level as renew. Elara braces against the pull, cataloguing the dangers: public scrutiny, the ever-present shadow of the Brotherhood, the scars he cannot hide. It would be easier, she argues with herself, to withdraw, to be nothing more than the sturdy tutor Nova leans on.

But it is no longer enough. Honesty demands she acknowledge the hunger for more—a hunger that terrifies her even as it beckons.

Nova turns, hands dusted with sand, face luminous with contentment. "Can I read to them now?" Her laughter bubbles up, feather-light.

Elara offers a smile, gentle and aching at the edges, sunlight trembling across her cheek. She nods, tucking away her decision for another moment, letting Nova's joy fill the study with hope unraveled from fear.

The kitchen glows under discreet strips of blue-white LED light, the air tinted with the scent of black pepper and caramelizing onions. Steel and glass surfaces reflect fragments of city lights bleeding through the windows, but tonight, it's the steady clack of knife against cutting board that keeps tension at bay. Orion lingers at the marble island, sleeves pushed to the elbow, demonstrating a chef's grip with a bell pepper in one hand as Elara, arms folded and gaze skeptical, surveys him from the opposite side.

He lifts a piece of radiant red flesh. "See, you're mangling it. Ridges facing down, not up." His voice is playful—unfamiliar ground, worn tentatively—and he nudges a pile of mismatched slices closer. "Granted, there's an art to destroying food too, but I haven't seen this particular... technique." He arches an eyebrow, jaw set in mock solemnity.

Elara snorts, rolling her eyes. "You complain, but you're the one who nearly set the smoke alarm off with toast yesterday. If you burn these, I'm ordering takeout and Nova gets to pick—last time she picked sushi pizza, and you looked like you'd seen the apocalypse." Her smile unfolds, and for a moment, the metallic sheen of the penthouse kitchen softens around her.

He grins, hands surrendered, glancing at her with a flicker of gratitude that barely escapes the droll surface. "Fine, go on. Chop however you want. Just don't blame me when half the salad's missing fingers." His words fade into the low hum of the city; laughter lingers, carving out new territory where, once, only silence lived.

She slides the knife back, their hands brushing as she reaches for a lemon. He feels that accidental contact more surely than the pulse in his wrists, a static promise in the space between them.

Past dinners rise, unbidden: memory shadows pooling behind the glass-and-steel decor. Cold, silent meals where he sat at this very table with Nova, both retreating into uneasy quiet after the shriek of headlines or the fallout of yet another phone call that fractured the day. He recalls the mechanical clatter of silverware, Nova's questions curled into her lap, wary to disturb the adult storm. Elara's arrival changed little at first—she'd sit across from him, posture precise, the unsaid stretching between them like thread drawn taut. He'd retreat behind sarcasm or silence, always certain his chaos would swallow any chance at ordinary comfort.

But tonight, the act of cooking is a dance, unhurried and experimental. There are small mishaps: a bell pepper slips, a sliver falls to the ground, Elara's laugh close enough he nearly forgets everything else. Somehow, in this repetition of normal, he senses a shift—a slow thawing of the ice that clung to every shared evening before.

By the time dinner is plated, the world outside is violet and gold, dusk swallowing the bright restlessness of day. They sit at the glass table; Orion's heart pounds a beat out of step with his carefully chosen calm. Beneath the glossy surface, reflections ripple—the city, Elara, him, all fractured, all contained within these four high walls.

She takes a bite, tilts her head, searching his face. "It's edible," she says, as if this is a rare feat in his kitchen.

He manages a huff of amusement but can't avoid the weight that returns when conversation stutters into realness. He grips his fork, eyes on the simple meal between them. "Elara, you ever feel like it'll all collapse? That no matter how much you plan... it isn't enough?" The words escape softer than intended. "Sometimes I look at Nova and I—every instinct says to run, fix something, bolt before I break us both. And then she says something little, like asking for another bedtime story, and I feel like a fraud. Like I'm pretending to be someone she needs." His thumb flicks against the table, an old tic betraying nerves. "I'm scared I'll never be enough for her. Or for anyone."

She's quiet, fingers curled around her glass. Then she puts it down, gaze steady. "It's not about enough, Orion. It's about showing up. Trying again, even if you fail half the time." Her voice, usually clipped with efficiency, is gentle. "You think Nova needs perfect? She asks for stories because you're there. You could burn every meal and it wouldn't matter, as long as you stay." Her hand crosses the table, palm open, inviting. "You're not alone in this."

He searches her face—only honesty there, and for once, he lets the truth find him. "I don't want to be," he says, not quite a plea.

Her thumb brushes the back of his hand, warmth spreading through skin and bone. The city's glow flickers along the window, silent, merciful.

It isn't a grand declaration—just hands entwined and plates cooling on the table, the hush as thick with hope as with things unspoken. In that brief, suspended moment, the old ghosts of clattering forks and unshed words step aside, leaving only the sound of their breath and a shared promise, tentative but real. When Orion squeezes Elara's hand, he knows it: this—whatever it is—matters more than fear.

Elara sits perched on the edge of her bed, legs curled beneath her as the city stretches far below, an endless constellation of cold gold and blue reflected in the glass. The late hour hushes even the penthouse's machinery; only the subtle hum of the vent and the distant thrum of rain against the windows keep her company. She twists the corner of the blanket between her fingers, her gaze roving the skyline that now feels less like a fortress and more like a question.

Her mind drifts, untethered, swept back through corridors lined with uneasy memories. Nights in a cramped apartment smelling of scorched coffee and burnt toast, the shape of disappointment in a lover's voice: "Too rigid, Elara. You hold back." She hears the slamming of doors—real and figurative—memories pulsing with every uncertain decision, each misstep that carved deeper lines between herself and trust. There were patterns, she recognizes now, webs of defense spun so painstakingly that even kindness couldn't always unravel them. The ghosts of old loves and old betrayals linger, hovering at the edge of her consciousness.

But tonight, their edges soften, blurred by newer images spilling tentatively into the spaces between her ribs. Orion in the living room, shadows etched behind his eyes as he peeled back his armor, words raw in the lamplight: I'm scared I'll fail Nova. The whiskey glass trembling ever so slightly in his hand—vulnerability from a man who clawed order from chaos, who expected the storm to bow to his will. Nova's arms tight around Elara's waist at bedtime, whispering, "Don't go yet." The laughter at dinner, the touch of possibility skimming Orion's voice.

She wonders, in this hush, if she could let herself anchor here, among the turbulence. What would it mean to belong, not by contractual obligation, not chained by duty, but by the volition of her own pulse? The city is vast, but the hugeness of it shrinks beneath the weight of this question. Could she wake each morning in the penthouse—sunlight fracturing across the marble—knowing this family, strange and storm-tossed, also needs her, also wants her?

She recalls the look in Orion's eyes when the laughter faded and only truth remained, how he waited—not for her to fix him, but simply to stay. To witness his fear, to cradle it alongside her own. Elara presses closer to the window, feeling the cooling glass leech the warmth from her skin, grounding her. Maybe she is, in her own way, as adrift as Orion, learning how to build shelter from the same storm.

If she let herself step into this world, really step in, what would it cost her? Old scars ache with warning—there will be more losses, more fractures, more nights alone with only the city to keep counsel. But underneath, old hopes flutter, stubborn and persistent as the first breath after a summer thunderclap. She craves, desperately, the thing she's denied herself most: to matter, to be chosen, not as a safe harbor but as something essential. A fixture in the chaos.

Outside, lightning flickers on the horizon, silent for now. Elara's chest tightens, but the fear doesn't paralyze; instead, it wakes something fighting to break free. Could she stand through the next storm, not because she's unfeeling, but because she's willing to risk being undone? Could vulnerability be its own kind of strength?

The world, poised on the edge of tomorrow, offers no answers. Still, resolve blooms in the quiet. She wraps herself tightly in the blanket, a shield and a promise, determined not to flee at the first sign of darkness. She stares out, lungs rising and falling, heart beating its silent tattoo—a language of longing, of reckless hope. Whatever comes, she will not run from these tangled threads of love, not now.

Footsteps pad softly down the hall—Nova's, hesitant, pausing at her door. Elara waits, half hoping for the small knock, half dreading it. After a moment, the footsteps retreat, and the penthouse quiets once more, intimacy and solitude blending into something close to peace.

Elara lifts her phone from the nightstand, thumbs hovering over the keyboard as words form and evaporate. She lets it fall instead, pressing her palm to the cool glass, the city's glittering arteries pulsing beneath her touch. Somewhere below, people chase refuge, meaning, warmth—even if it means standing in the path of their own storms.

A memory surfaces—her mother singing softly as rain rattled the roof of their childhood home, a lullaby about not fearing thunder, for it always passed, and something green always grew from the wreckage. Elara feels the ache of nostalgia twine with fierce, embryonic hope.

Her eyes sting, and she lets the tears fall, silent and hot, their presence both confession and release. The pain mingles with possibility, fear with anticipation. She does not shy from it, not anymore. She presses her forehead to the glass, breath fogging a halo on the pane.

Tonight, the future is uncertain, molten with threat and promise. But for the first time, Elara lets herself picture a life shaped not by defenses, but by the courage to begin, even if the storm surges again. Her tears—salt on her lips—bear quiet witness to the hope blooming cautiously inside her, as the city keeps vigil, pulsing and alive beneath her window.

Temptation and Misunderstanding

Afternoon light dims through the library nook's glass, reflecting pinpricks of city gold across polished marble. Elara presses Nova's slim workbook closed, her fingers brushing the edges of a shyly drawn hermit crab, and watches, for a moment, as Nova gathers her pencils and pads them away in her coral-knit bag. The air smells faintly of lavender and graphite. When Nova slips down the hallway toward the pet terrarium, Elara's phone buzzes in her palm. She hesitates—teaching always meant silencing distractions—and almost ignores it. Then a chill prickles her arms. The number blinking on the screen feels like a ghost. She swipes to answer, her voice barely steady, knowing Nova can hear nothing with the study doors muffled shut behind her.

"Hello?"

A rush of static comes from the other end. He sounds just as she remembers: measured, clipped, thoughts always proceeding two beats ahead. He wastes no pleasantries.

"Elara. It's important. I need a word."

Her eyes dart to the clock between art prints reflecting Orion's world: twelve-hour days, fractal urgency.

"I can't," she manages, aware of the weight in her chest. He slips in sideways, always, his old talent for finding the crack in her defenses.

"Meet me for coffee. I won't keep you long—unless you'd rather talk here, while your employer listens in?"

No place feels safe, suddenly. She glances at Nova's closed door, torn.

"Fine. Half an hour."

City dusk presses down like rain as she steps through side streets to the café, rain-slicked glass beading with light from flickering tea lamps. The place is nearly empty. Cinnamon and scorched beans churn in the dimness, and muddled red light from the half-drawn blinds stains the pressed linen of her coat. He sits alone, every inch the courtroom's darling: suit immaculate, fingers drumming a legal rhythm on the table, chair chosen for the best line of sight to the exit. She doesn't take off her coat.

He gets up just enough to look polite. There's a smile, but it doesn't reach his eyes.

"You got my message. You look... tired."

She sits.

"It's been a week," Elara says, her voice neutral.

A server approaches. She waves off the offer of pastry and orders black coffee. Her ex does the same, his gaze flicking briefly to her hands.

"This isn't social," he says quietly, leaning forward. "There's opportunity here, Elara. For both of us."

She's silent, her stomach tight, heart thudding. He always was blunt when he wanted to unsettle her.

He lowers his voice.

"You're living with Orion Vega now. Let's not pretend that isn't valuable."

She bristles, heat rising in her cheeks.

"I'm Nova's tutor, not a—"

He cuts her off, his voice smooth.

"Doesn't matter what you call it. You're on the inside. Everyone's circling that family, waiting for someone to slip. If you had information about his company—anything—it could change things for you. For me. Maybe you need insurance in case that loyalty blows up in your face."

Her hand curls around the coffee cup—still untouched, the rim icy beneath her skin.

"I don't operate like that. I'm here for Nova."

His smile sharpens, just a flick of teeth.

"That's admirable. Noble, even. But how long until he lets you go, Elara? He's reckless. You know it. Word is, the board wants him out, and you're just—collateral. Wouldn't you like something of your own before this ends?"

Old memories prickle: late nights stacked with legal briefs, him quizzing her between kisses, ambition coiling through their talk like smoke. She'd envied his certainty, his drive—until winning became more important to him than loving.

The conversation in the café seems at once distant and too close, his voice echoing with the warning of decisions already made and gone wrong. He offers hypotheticals: a slip of conversation at breakfast, a list of names Nova mentions. Harmless things, repackaged as "leverage." The pressure isn't overt but insinuates itself into every pause.

Elara meets his gaze, her own face set.

"I told you. I'm not interested."

He nods, almost regretful, but pushes again.

"You're not safe there, Elara. All it takes is one rumor, one mistake, and you'll lose your job—or maybe worse. You could make a new start. I could help. All it takes is a little honesty."

Her words are tight:

"Honesty isn't currency. Not with children's lives."

He relaxes, leaning back, but his voice is soft with warning.

"It's an option anyway. For when you need it. I'll be waiting."

The coffee—now cold—sits between them as evening presses up against swollen windows. She gathers her bag, hands trembling in the shadowed light. As she rises, memories knot in her throat: ambition, love, separation. Every choice a ledger against trust.

"Goodnight," she manages.

He barely looks up.

"My offer stands, Elara. Call me when you're ready."

She steps out, coat pressed to her, rain tapping a warning across the pavement as city lights snag in every puddle. She moves through the growing dark, fear and guilt still knotted deep inside, and wonders if there is safe ground left for someone standing between storms.

Orion's footsteps echo off damp pavement, city lights smearing silver and gold across the windshields of parked cars. He leaves the pulse of the boardroom behind, hunger and expense reports crowding his head, the battery of his phone still warm from relentless notifications. The air is cool, laced with the faintest whiff of ozone and exhaust, yet the city's anxiety has not seeped so deeply into him as it does now—when he catches, out of the corner of his eye, a familiar silhouette through a half-open café window.

Elara, all clean lines and poise even in casual shadow, sits across from a hulking figure with the posture of a man who expects every word to become evidence. Glass lanterns dance across their faces, casting blue shadows against cheap paneled walls and sticky tabletops yet to be wiped for the night. The sidewalk beneath Orion's boots hums as a tram clatters by, peeling a strip of orange light across the rain-streaked window.

He stops. Hands bury in jacket pockets, thumb pressing to the faint scar on his arm—unthinking, familiar. He watches Elara lean forward, earnest, a tension in her shoulders he has learned to identify as the raw edge of honesty or restraint. Across from her, the prosecutor sits at calculated ease. The man radiates that particular city-law confidence: chin up, eyes sharp, suit free of lint despite the grime drifting in off the street.

The world outside condenses to the hush of them behind glass. Orion's chest tightens. Even through the barrier, he feels the heat and collision, something definitive passing between those two heads bowed together. His mind races. Is it worry? Or is it something he can't bear to voice?

Slack face, stiff jaw, he looks away—then back. Elara nods at something, a jerky motion unlike her usual control, while the ex's fingers tap out a lawyer's code against the cracked ceramic crockery, relentless as the seconds ticking down in court.

A gust from a passing car shifts the café's door open a crack, the city's throb pulsing in. Snatches of their conversation filter across the thinning night. "Leverage," the ex says, the word sliding out with a lawyer's chill. Pause. "Protection. Opportunity, Elara. What's the point of standing by if you're not going to use the cards you've been dealt?"

Elara says nothing—at least nothing Orion can hear through the fractured city song and the steady drip of late rain off the eaves. Her hands move on the table, slender fingers wrapping hard around her mug, knuckles paling with the kind of pressure Orion remembers from boardrooms and bedside apologies. Betrayal. The ex spits the word out in a low, clean rhythm. Orion's pulse surges so violently he tastes copper. His skin prickles beneath the folds of his jacket.

He reels, caught in a silent war between wanting to storm through the glass and knowing he can't—won't—be that man, the one who shows his own wounds too plainly. Instinct makes him step backward, the city's noises rising to fill the empty space left by trust eroding just out of sight.

His thoughts spiral, conjuring swift, brutal futures. He sees Elara slipping into the shadows of the penthouse, clutching some damning secret gleaned over homework and evening tea. He imagines her voice caught on an intercepted call, selling out the empty rooms where his sister once laughed. He even pictures his own name sealed on some prosecutor's file, Nova's guardianship slipping through his fingers while the world records every failure, every misstep. He knows how these things go. He has witnessed empires fall on whispers and fractured allegiances—knows the cost of believing in anyone who wasn't forced to stay.

"Why should I let her in?" he thinks, teeth clenched against the taste of loss. "Why should I pretend she—anyone—would choose this storm if there was a way out? Everyone wants something. Even the ones who swear they don't."

His mind turns on itself, cycling through memories both sharp and blurred. Lovers who chased the glow of his money and the crash of his chaos—gone, leaving splinters behind. Friends who flinched when the world turned ugly, board members who smiled too wide before voting him out of his own meeting. And here is Elara—practical, honest Elara—talking to a man whose profession is weaponizing the truth.

His heart wants to believe she wouldn't. That she's here for Nova, for the faint, trembling hope of something like family. Still, the seed of doubt takes root, watered by exhaustion and the fear that every moment of stability is only a prelude to disaster. He closes his eyes, lashes damp from the city mist, and lets the ache carve through him.

Across the street, the café lights flicker as the server begins to stack chairs, shadow engulfing half the room. Orion sees Elara's eyes move—maybe searching, maybe just tired. Before she or her ex can see him, he turns on his heel, boots striking out a rhythm of retreat. His reflection gleams for a split second in a puddle: hard jaw, eyes storm-dark.

A black sedan idles quietly at the curb, the driver wisely silent as Orion slides into the backseat. Cold leather presses against his spine. As the city peels away behind tinted glass, Orion's thoughts loop on themselves—leverage, protection, betrayal—a litany that cuts deeper with each repetition. He fists his hands and stares out at the skyline as dusk sets the world aflame. The penthouse window calls him home, but the warmth is gone; all that waits inside is the certainty that even hope can be weaponized.

Orion pushes through the penthouse door, the city's rain-soaked wind still clinging to his clothes. The black German Shepherd lifts its head, eyes shining from the shadow at the threshold, but Orion only glances sidelong and turns away, his jaw tight. Light from the hallway slips over his shoes, painting his path in fractured, bluish lines.

Elara steps softly from the dimness of the living room. She hesitates, one hand against her arm, lips pressing together at the brittle set of Orion's shoulders. "You're late," she manages, her voice gentle, but in the hush hangs something hopeful, waiting for permission to breathe.

He doesn't give it. "Had things to do," he says, crumpling his coat over the back of the nearest chair. His tone cuts the air, thin and cold, then he strides past her toward the kitchen, the Shepherd trailing a few careful steps behind before curling again by the lounge.

Elara follows, nerves stitched tight inside her chest. Orion doesn't look at her as he sorts through the stack of mail, papers flicking too hard against the marble, the hard-edged clatter filling the silence between them.

"Long day?" she tries again, her voice low. "Everything go all right at the meeting?"

"Fine," Orion answers, not meeting her eyes. He thumbs bills aside, tossing an envelope toward the pile. "Everything's just fine."

She stands across from him, catching the venom in his clipped answers, the way his eyes focus intently on anything but her presence. The kitchen's glow pools gold around them, catching the shine of stainless steel and the tautness in his cheeks. His hands shake, only lightly, but she sees it.

"Orion—" Elara's words come careful, but strong. "Don't do this. If something's wrong, say it. I can't help if you keep shutting me out."

He laughs—a hollow sound, echoing off glass and stone. "Why would I need help, Elara? You're only here for Nova, remember?" His sarcasm skims the surface, but anger warps beneath, brittle and raw. "How much do you plan on helping, anyway? You and your... friends outside the house?"

Her brows knit in confusion, the first real hint of fear entering her gaze. "What are you talking about? Did something happen?"

"Oh, plenty happens," Orion snaps. Shadows gather sharply under his eyes. "Funny thing, hearing words like leverage and betrayal drifting from a conversation you weren't supposed to overhear. Makes a man wonder just how close his circle really is. Or how much his so-called help is actually helping."

A thousand retorts swirl through Elara's mind, panic mixing with defensiveness. "I met with an old friend. That's all. It wasn't— He wanted something from me, Orion. I wouldn't—"

"So you admit it," Orion's voice cuts across hers. "You're meeting with prosecutors now? In secret cafés? Gearing up to sell what, exactly? My trust? Nova's safety? Or is it just whatever scraps you think you can pull from my so-called empire before it burns down around us all?"

Her fists clench at her sides, nails digging crescents into her palms. "Stop twisting this! I'm not here to hurt you or Nova. I don't owe you blind faith, Orion—not with how much of my own life's on the line every day in this place!"

He slams a palm down on the countertop, paper fluttering to the floor. "So now you're the victim? You get to have secrets, but I'm just supposed to hand mine over? That's not how this works, Elara. Not in my house."

She straightens, breathing hard, anger and heartbreak warping her tone. "No, it isn't. But if you want me to act like some loyal dog, take your commands and never question, you picked the wrong woman. I came for Nova. I'm still here for her. And for you—if you could see past your paranoia for one moment."

"That's rich," Orion spits. He can see rain streaking the windows—a dim, wet world blurring beyond the penthouse glass. "You talk about trust, but you're the one making deals in the dark."

She presses her hands flat to the counter to steady herself. "This isn't about trust; it's about honesty. You won't let anyone in—not if you can't control what happens next."

He glares at her, fighting the tremor of something unspeakable in his chest. "Better to keep control than get stabbed in the back. That's how people survive in my world." He averts his eyes, shoulders caving inward with shame and rage. He can't let her see; can't let her know the place where grief needles so deep it feels like marrow.

Stillness settles. The hush between them is dense, swollen with anger and all the words neither dare to utter. Orion's mouth works soundlessly, then, suddenly, he storms out—shoulders squared, feet pounding the marble, leaving Elara behind, blinking back stinging tears.

She doesn't call after him. She stands in the gold-lit ruin of their kitchen, breath trembling, heart aching, watching as every fragile tie between them strains under the weight of suspicion and pride.

Somewhere down the hall, a door slams. The German Shepherd, pressed silent against the living room shadows, lifts its head and lets out a low, uncertain whine. The penthouse lies heavy, as if even the city has stopped breathing.

Rain patterns against the floor-to-ceiling windows, cast in wavering streaks by the silver gleam of the city's distant neon. The penthouse dining room is a hush of polished marble and low gold lighting, shadows pressed to the corners. Nova sits at the end of the long table, her feet barely reaching the rung of her chair, eyes flickering between Elara and Orion. Their plates are artfully arranged—steamed vegetables, grilled salmon, a hint of lemon still lingering in the air. But the food is untouched, cooling under the weight of a silence that hums with tension.

Orion leans on one elbow, his gaze trained on nothing, his stare hollow and far off in the glass. The city's light sprawls beneath him, but his shoulders stay locked, mouth a rigid line, hands working the fork in restless circles. Elara sits upright, napkin folded into an angular, defensive shield on her lap. Her smile appears and vanishes so quickly it feels like seeing a reflection on water, fragile and easily broken.

Nova tucks a strand of hair behind her ear, her fork tracing the rim of her plate. Beneath the gleaming bulbs, the movement barely stirs the air. Every so often, she glances from Elara's stilled hands to Orion's steely profile, searching for a flicker, any sign their words might finally cut through the cold between them.

"Would you maybe..." Nova's voice is soft, tentative; she picks at invisible lint on her sleeve and continues, "... want to play a board game after dinner?" She tries to catch Elara's eye first, then Orion's, casting the hope like a lifeline. The words seem to land on water, sending tremors across the silence. Elara's fingers hesitate mid-reach, eyes darting toward Nova. Orion's jaw moves, a silent tick.

Elara sets her fork down, reaching across the table to place her hand over Nova's—a gentle touch, all warmth nestled in trembling restraint. "I'd like that," she says. Her voice tries for brightness, but something brittle scrapes beneath the surface. Nova feels the rasp, the way the smile doesn't touch Elara's eyes. She presses her palm back, clinging to the contact for as long as she can, before Elara's hand retreats.

Orion's response comes a beat too late and is edged with weariness. "Sure, kiddo," he mumbles, eyes snagging on the shifting shadows beyond the windows. His fork skims over the salmon, pushing it into cold flakes. He never looks at either of them, his attention fractured by something silent and urgent. The space between them stays filled with things unsaid, the scent of cool lemon and damp wool rising from Elara's sleeve the only thing alive.

Nova's disappointment settles like a shadow at her feet. She wanted laughter, the jostle of game pieces, the shimmer of ordinary happiness. Yet the table is an island, the sea between her and her guardians raw with invisible storms.

She gathers her plate and stands, moving quietly to the kitchen. The marble is cool under her toes. She rinses her plate as water runs sharp and cold over her fingers, distantly aware of Elara's voice fluttering in the background, low and careful. Orion, silent, leaves his own plate unfinished, steps measured and heavy as he crosses to the living room.

Nova dries her hands on the edge of her skirt, her heart fluttering against the small bones of her chest. She catches her reflection in the window, a pale shimmer against the press of rain. The world outside is a kaleidoscope of city lights, haloes blurred, the storm swelling beyond the glass. She leans into the pane, cool and trembling under her forehead, and listens.

She carries so many memories of rooms heavy with the echoes of grown-up voices—sharp, breaking, rising and falling in rhythms she learned to dread when her mother was sick and every night throbbed with uncertainty. That sense lingers: the ache of things falling apart, her hands too small to gather the pieces. The old fear tugs at her even now, whispering that everything good might slip away.

But Nova holds hope, fragile as a flame caught between cupped hands. She tries to fit herself into the silent spaces, believing if she can bridge the gap—one gentle word, one game, one touch—then maybe the storm won't pull them apart. Maybe she can remind them both what family feels like, pieced together from longing and grief and something quietly fierce.

As she stands by the window, rain tracing pathways down the glass, Nova closes her eyes and makes a promise only the storm and the city can hear. She will believe, even when no one else can. She will be the thread. She will hold fast to the love she knows is there, shimmering beneath all the silence and sorrow, and she will wait for them to find their way back to her—however long the thunder takes to clear.

Gala Shadows

Seraphina's silhouette spills across the polished marble as she steps into the penthouse, the sunset bleeding amber and plum through the floor-to-ceiling windows. She moves with the assurance of someone born to glide through city storms, her presence sparking an electric anticipation in the quiet hush after a day spent dodging press calls. In her hand, a gilt-edged envelope glimmers—a sigil, a summons, an elegant demand.

"Elara. It's time."

The invitation's paper is cold between Elara's fingertips—a weight carrying with it the hush of expectation and the icy hum of risk. The card has the precision of a knife's edge, embossed with the swirling emblem of a world defined by watching itself in mirrored surfaces. Seraphina's eyes flicker, direct and warm, as she draws Elara aside, lowering her voice just enough that the penthouse's digital hush—a background symphony of devices quietly sifting through Orion's crises—seems to soften.

"The board's nerves are frayed. Everyone's watching. You need to be seen tonight. Not as the help, but as his equal. Trust me—it matters."

Elara doesn't answer right away. She watches her own face in the mirror later, as twilight spills over the city and presses shadows into the hollows of her cheeks. The dress Seraphina brings is simple, dark navy silk, skimming her frame—modest but luminous, so unlike her utilitarian workwear. Each motion—threading the braid, pinning stray curls—feels like crafting armor from silk and resolve. She remembers the echo of Orion and Nova's argument the night before: Nova's panicked breath, Orion's voice raised, everything—her role here, her belonging—suddenly loose and unsteady.

She smooths the dress, thinks of the storm within the penthouse walls and the sharper one outside. Somewhere in the city, the elite swirl in ecosystems of power where truth is currency, and the right smile can upend the night's balance. Reputation, to these people, isn't just armor—it's the bone holding everything upright. One careless slip, and the machine of rumor grinds even the powerful into ash.

Orion appears at her doorway, the hush between them cut by the faint click of his watch. He's changed from chaos into composure: navy suit crisp, dark hair meticulously controlled, only the restless set of his mouth betraying the strain beneath his skin.

"You're ready?" His words are smooth, practiced. A pause—then, softer—"You don't have to like any of this. But I need you beside me tonight. We control the narrative—at least until they decide to rewrite it."

She nods, meets his gaze in the half-light, searching for cracks in the mask. For Nova, she tells herself. For all the secrets that whisper beneath the marble floors. For the chance—just maybe—to anchor her own truth inside this riptide.

They enter the ballroom side by side. The city's upper echelons glimmer in cascading light, dresses and suits spilling color and motion across a marble ocean. Crystal chandeliers refract the spectrum overhead; perfume and champagne combine into an intoxicating fog, dense with the hush of expectations barely spoken. Cameras flare the second Orion steps from shadow into center stage. Flashbulbs pop in bursts, trapping them in a sequence of sharp-edged tableaux: Orion's hand hovering just above the small of her back; Elara, poised and unsmiling, her fingers smoothing invisible creases from the silk. For one bracing instant, she realizes the entire room has turned as if to synchronize itself to the rumors already seething in tomorrow's headlines.

Inside this world, rituals matter. Every gesture, every glance is a calculated offering—to donors, to rivals, to the gods of public opinion. Scandal is more than embarrassment; it poisons contracts, breaks alliances, and reshapes fortunes overnight. The city's elite play for consequence, and the fallout is swift, merciless. Recovery means finding the exact pitch of grace and cunning, never wavering, never allowing the mask to slip.

Elara moves through clusters of jewel-toned conversations where laughter lingers like cologne, masking calculation. She feels the whispered judgments grazing her bare skin. Their eyes linger, noting every detail: the simplicity of her gown, the braid pulled with the precision of a schoolmistress, the unfashionable honesty with which she defers flattery. Every question is a test; every smile, a blade. Seraphina floats past on silk slippers, redirecting pointed inquiries, framing Elara not as an outsider but as an asset—a woman poised at the cusp of power.

"But of course, darling," Seraphina says, a subtle nod drawing attention away from hot topics, "Elara's discipline is exactly what children in our city need." The script hovers between sincerity and performance, every phrase carrying the weight of a thousand unseen consequences.

"Are you always this calm?" Elara murmurs when Seraphina returns.

"Only when I know the sharks are hungry."

A thin smile flickers on Seraphina's lips. She draws Elara aside just long enough for the crowd to sweep on.

"Shoulders back. Don't let them decide who you are. But tonight—every move counts. We make them believe you belong here, and maybe you will." Her eyes are gentle, flinty beneath the kindness. "I'll be close if you need a rescue."

For a breath, Elara stands at the edge of light and shadow, the ballroom's hum pressing close. Her pulse keeps time with the sparkle of crystal and the knowledge that one wrong glance can tilt all their precarious worlds.

Mariel finds Elara in a cluster of shadows, where the light from the wall-high gallery windows leaks in thin, expressionist rectangles. Abstract paintings crane from their gilded hooks, all vibrant color and fractured geometry, as though the whole room is holding its breath beneath the weight of silk gowns and muted orchestral strings from the distant ballroom. Elara's fingers brush the glossy margin of a canvas, but her eyes are elsewhere—tracking the rise and fall of voices at the gallery entrance, the shimmer of a sequined dress here, a clipped laugh there. Every detail collides: the faint scent of white lilies, too sweet and suffocating; the soft, predatory swish of polished shoes over marble.

Mariel's touch is feather-light on Elara's forearm, her voice angled low and sharp as broken glass. "Come with me."

She guides Elara behind an overgrown arrangement of orchids. For an instant, they're invisible—shields in a kaleidoscopic garden of shadow, where petals exhale their lush, waxy perfume. Mariel's gaze flickers over each guest, cataloging faces, names, allegiances.

"Listen—this is important," Mariel murmurs, spine taut, heels planted as if bracing against an unseen wind. "Helios has eyes everywhere tonight. Two of the media partners from Orion's last product launch? They're here. And they're not alone."

Elara's breath catches, shallow in her chest. The last hour had already been a balancing act—performing calm assurance as whispers darted just out of earshot, hands pressing champagne flutes with practiced grace, lips curled in polite smiles that felt like masks borrowed from strangers. The threat Mariel names sends fissures up her resolve.

Mariel keeps her gaze fixed beyond Elara's shoulder, lips barely moving. "The stories in the press? They're planting them. They're orchestrating which rumors bleed into the daylight. Worse, they're paying for access. You see a cocktail in the wrong hand, a notepad sticking from a clutch, you do not speak."

Elara nods, pulse knotting beneath the fragile bone of her throat. It's not the first time she's been forced to read a room like a battlefield—Nova's panic attacks trained her well for microexpressions: the twist in a mouth, shoulders angled away, eyes darting in search of escape or opportunity. Memories resurface in jagged montages. The night Nova shuttered herself in a closet at the estate, drawing in short bursts of air while Darius counted each inhale, slow and grounding. The press hounds outside the garden wall, voices amplified through megaphones, eager to pounce on even Nova's stumbling laugh. Instinct has become a lifeline, her shield for both child and self.

Mariel leans in, her words a hiss. "There are at least three people here I'd bet work for Helios. I saw one of them watching you and Orion earlier, jotting on their phone each time you so much as blinked. And that man by the bronze sculpture? He tried to grill me about Nova. Has he spoken to you?"

A memory blinks on—earlier, by the hors d'oeuvre table, a man with salt-and-pepper hair and a too-bright smile had asked, "She's adjusting to the city, I presume?" His gaze didn't pause for answers, already scanning the perimeter for more.

Elara's voice is steady now. "He asked about Nova. About her school hours. I thought nothing of it. Should I report him to security?"

Mariel's eyes narrow, her tone closer to steel than comfort. "Don't make a scene—just stay with Seraphina or me. Helios looks for divides, for moments when no one's paying attention." She pulls back and smooths a stray strand of hair behind her ear. "If you sense something off, tell me. Trust your instincts. They're why you're still standing."

Their eyes meet, and Elara feels the warning vibrate down her spine like a struck chord. She turns, walking from their alcove with a practiced calm, heart hammering as she rejoins the shivering tide of partygoers. The air is thick, tinged with the metallic tang of anticipation and the sourness of expensive wine gathering in half-empty glasses. Her eyes move restlessly: evaluating, isolating, dismissing. She notices a cluster of socialites huddled near the bar, voices pitched too low, glances slicing sideways through the crowd. Cameras wink, hollow and mercenary, from the hands of men posing as guests.

She moves closer to Seraphina and Lila—there's safety in numbers, or at least in the choreography of well-rehearsed alliances. Seraphina trades her silent reassurance for a squeeze at Elara's elbow, grounding her for an instant. Lila's eyes sweep the gallery, gentle but alert, the soft arch of her brow spelling out her question: Are you okay?

All around them, the gallery pulses: laughter, music, the scent of melting beeswax from the candelabras, the flash and retreat of paparazzi under strict orders to remain invisible until the mask slips. Elara stands straighter, searching for the crack in the surface.

Her scan lands on a tall man in a navy velvet jacket—his posture too rigid, his gaze fixed. The moment her attention sharpens, he turns away, disappearing behind a wall of glittering shoulders, leaving a ripple of unease that crawls down her skin.

Elara's vigilance stretches tight, every sense tuned to the frequency of danger. Tonight, she realizes, requires more than poise and pretty answers. It demands every hard-won instinct she's ever earned.

Orion's penthouse office is carved from flickers of city neon and the soft drone of distant thunder. The party sheen hasn't worn off: his collar is still crisp, the scent of vetiver and Elara's subtle perfume still clings to his jacket, but the hush that falls here is edged, uneasy. His assistant—young, nervous, still in her own borrowed gala shoes—hovers at the threshold with a thick stack of envelopes and a tablet, bright icons twitching against the glass. On his desk, the holographic display casts blue light over a mountain of unopened messages; every headline pulses with his name, Elara's, and that word: scandal.

For a moment, Orion stands in silence, jaw tense, gaze fixed on the city. His reflection in the window looks hollowed out, caught somewhere between the sharp angles of a man who once commanded storms and the weary shadow of someone hiding from them. His phone buzzes. The board is already waiting. He taps to answer, switching to speaker, voice low with practiced calm—the mask he saves for damage control.

"We're not here to discuss rumors," Orion says, trying for steel but finding only echo. "We're here to discuss the fund's projections."

"What's the point if the foundation itself is bleeding?" shoots back the head of legal, her tone brittle as glass. "Vega, this story's everywhere. This—" and a headline leaks through the call, editor's choice in urgent crimson: Vega Caught in Secret Romance Amid Custody Risk. "Investors are worried. So are we."

"They'll settle down," Orion lies, flicking his eyes to the growing flood in his inbox—another investor, another demand for clarity, another seed of doubt. He drums his fingers beside a photo of Nova, resisting the urge to snarl.

Finance chimes in, cool and remote. "Sentiment is shifting. The board expects decisive action. The custody hearing is in days. The optics—"

Orion's hand tightens. "Optics change. I change them." The room tastes of metal and ozone; the city's pulse, once a comfort, now feels like a warning. On the periphery, Elara stands by the glass coffee table, her hands folded. She is backlit by city glare, unreadable, yet her posture is unmoving—unafraid, or unwilling to show fear. He wonders if she ever feels it.

The call grinds on, pressure mounting with each word uttered as if he were the one on trial. When the board disconnects, the office falls into electric quiet. Orion rubs the knot at his temple, a pained, restless gesture, and then snags his tablet from the assistant's outstretched hand. She vanishes without a sound.

Headlines leap and mutate: VEGA AND THE TUTOR—TOO CLOSE FOR COMFORT? Snapshots from the gala—his hand at Elara's back, Elara's lips parted mid-laugh, their eyes locked against the world's lens. He scrolls through a deluge of speculation, each image sharpened by the firestorm of anonymous opinions. Below the photos, the comments bloom: Is she after his money? Another predator? Or just his daughter's replacement mother?

Elara silently moves closer, shoulders squared. He senses her presence with every frayed nerve, aware that her calm has become the one constant in an ocean of shifting loyalties.

He whips his phone down to the marble with a low curse. "They're judging every blink, every breath. All for a story they don't understand."

"I see the headlines, Orion. But I don't care what they say about me," Elara replies. Her tone is matter-of-fact, no tremor, no attempt at comfort—just an unshakable line drawn in the air between them. "I'm here for Nova, and I'm not leaving. You're not the only one who wants to keep her safe."

He studies her, searching for cracks. She meets his gaze, strong as tempered glass. There's a question there—maybe fear, maybe faith. Orion can't afford to pick the wrong answer.

"You think it's that simple? You think loyalty's enough when the wrong rumor could put Nova in the system?" His words snap, bitter, but the desperation beneath is unmistakable.

Elara's chin tips up. "No, I know it isn't simple. I also know you're not alone, no matter how much you pretend to be." She doesn't flinch as the city's light glances off her cheek. "Trust me, Orion. Just this once."

He breaks away first. "Get the staff out of here. I need... space." The edge of surrender in his voice is new, almost painful.

Elara disappears, quiet as starlight. One by one, the penthouse empties—shifting footsteps swallowed by marble and glass, until only Orion remains. He stands alone for a long beat, staring at his own hands, at the reflection twisted in the dark windows. In the hush, memories spiral: Nova's laughter muted by panic, his sister's smile vanishing at the edge of memory, every promise crushed beneath the weight of expectation.

He crosses the echoing space to his quarters, the hush swallowing even the sound of his breath. Inside, the air is cooler, scented faintly by the dark-leafed plant his sister tended, the one thing he's never let die. He drops onto the low couch, the city's moonlight painting silver on his suit, and pulls his sister's photo from the side table. Its worn edges dig into his palm as the hush grows heavy.

Images flash through his mind—Nova's teary eyes, Elara's unwavering calm. With the storm howling at his door, he wonders: how many more choices can he make before the world takes everything? What if all the defenses in the world can't keep her safe? What if he himself is the storm Nova needs shelter from?

Tonight, every private decision is another story waiting to be weaponized. Even his fear, even his hope, belong now to an audience waiting for him to slip. Orion clutches the photo until his knuckles whiten, alone with a city's scrutiny pressing in and the dread that this—this endless, spectral spotlight—might never let them breathe again.

Intrigue in the Air

Late sunlight spills gold over the marble-floored foyer as the elevator slides open. The distant hum of city traffic echoes faintly through the penthouse's glass walls, blurring the world below into a haze of glittering towers. A uniformed courier stands framed in the threshold, clipboard tucked beneath his arm like a shield. His cap is pulled low, eyes obscured, posture practiced. He offers a polite, rehearsed nod, transferring a compact wooden box into Orion Vega's waiting hands—a box polished as deep as aged mahogany, its metal accents glinting sharp and cold.

"No signature?" Orion's words are clipped and suspicious. The courier barely meets his gaze, shakes his head, and pivots to vanish into the elevator's mirrored maw. The doors close, swallowing him without so much as a goodbye. Silence settles, brittle as glass.

From the kitchen, the muted percussion of groceries—paper bags rustling, a carton tapped on stone—stutters to a halt. Elara Kent appears, sleeves rolled up, gaze tracking the box as Orion carries it past the foyer's blue-lit edges to the glass-topped table that anchors the living area. She wipes her palms on her skirt, the soft scent of thyme and fresh bread blending with a sterile whiff of lacquer from the box.

"Another present?" she asks, her voice even but wary. Her hands reach out before she can stop herself. The box is heavier than its size would suggest, strangely dense against her palms. She turns it, watching the light catch on hand-engraved script curling across the lid's surface: Every empire falls from within. Her thumb sweeps slowly over the letters, trying to read the secret pulse in the grain. There's a dull hollowness—a resonance that shouldn't be there—beneath the ornate carvings.

"No sender?" she asks, glancing up. Orion shrugs, lips compressed, eyes shifting between the box and the skyline beyond the windows.

He flicks the latch open. The hinges sigh, a sound too mechanical to be comforting. Inside, black velvet lines the compartment—a cushion for a delicate clockwork mechanism. With a twist, the mechanism clicks to life, releasing a brittle tune. The melody drifts through the air, notes sweet at first, then discordant, needle-fine and too fast, as if rushing toward a conclusion it can't avoid.

Elara tilts the box gently. A faint rattle shivers up through her hands—metal inside wood. Her fingers tense. "Hear that? Something's loose."

Orion is already stalking toward the kitchen drawers, retrieving a slim toolkit. He's motion and intent made flesh—crouching beside her, unscrewing the base with swift, decisive hands. Their shoulders nearly touch, the air thickening between them. Elara steadies the box while Orion pries away a hidden panel on the velvet lining.

A circuit-board transmitter stares up at them: spiral patterns etched in copper, microchips sewn like sequins into dark silk. An LED blinks in rapid, secretive code—red and insistent. Fear sharpens the moment, carving the room into raw edges.

Orion leans in, inspecting the serials. His posture stiffens, jaw tightening. "Custom hardware. This isn't some amateur trick. Whoever did this knows Brotherhood protocol—hell, it's an improved version of our own transmission security." His voice grows harsh, brittle as winter glass. "We're being taunted. Someone inside had to have supplied this. Maybe someone who was meant to protect us."

Elara draws back, lips pressed thin. Her gaze sweeps the skyline's reflections, then the room, as if expecting shadows to sprout from the glossy floor.

Orion lifts the device, anger simmering just beneath his skin. "They're in our home. Our sanctuary. This—" he gestures with the transmitter, "is a declaration. Not just surveillance—it's war, Elara."

She meets his gaze, her voice low but steady. "Don't leap, Orion. We don't know who. Not yet." She places the music box down at the far edge of the table, its song gone silent, but the echo of that mechanical melody seems to linger, woven into the penthouse's pulse.

He laughs then, the sound harsh and humorless. "You want to tell me this isn't one of ours betraying us? That this—this level of tech—is random? I can name five people with access."

"Maybe so. Or maybe you're playing into their hands by suspecting everyone at once. That's what they want, isn't it? Doubt, division. Slow poison." Her words are soft, razor-edged.

He looks away, running a hand through his hair, the city below a swirl of molten light and cold shadow.

The Brotherhood was meant to be impregnable—a fortress built on secrecy, loyalty, and unbreakable pacts sworn in blood and data alike. For years, threats came from beyond: rivals, hostile takeovers, feeble corporate spies with obsolete wires and cracked codes. But this is something else. This is a message as much as a weapon, a seamless fusion of art and sabotage. The box—beautiful, cryptic, intimate—slides across Orion's table like a chessmaster's opening gambit. Somewhere, an adversary is reaching deeper, proving the old rules unfit for a battlefield where trust is just another system to be exploited, where every alliance—every family—carries the potential to fracture from within.

The realization lands cold in Orion's gut, settling into old scars. Safety—the imagined haven he's carved from this skyline—was always a fragile illusion. Now, the walls wear eyes. The weight of Nova's future and the Brotherhood's survival presses heavier than ever, demanding vigilance, suspicion, and sacrifice. Every pulse in his veins beats with the demand to protect, but also with dread: every layer of security peeled back reveals one more threat, closer, smarter, possibly grown from within.

Elara's fingers linger on the table's edge. The box rests between them, silent but looming, as heavy as prophecy.

Orion bolts the study's door and snaps the blackout curtains closed. The city lights pressing at the window fade, replaced by the sterile white glow from overhead. The conference table's glass surface gleams, reflecting the stark anxiety stitched through the room. Security sweeps past outside—shadows moving with purpose, radios murmuring only barely audible through triple-insulated walls.

He props his phone on a matte black stand, its encrypted app already pinging the Brotherhood. Within moments, the screen splits: Caius's dark, controlled gaze from his loft, Lucien backlit by rows of law tomes, Darius appearing quietly resolute, sleeves rolled, the hint of exhaustion in his set jaw. The music box—its gleaming surfaces incongruously delicate in the war-room atmosphere—sits center stage. Orion pulls up high-res images on his tablet, cycling between the circuit board, the text burned into the lid, and the chilling pulse of the transmitter's red diode.

"Minutes ago. No return address. No sender," Orion starts flatly, showing them the thick, blocky engraving—Every empire falls from within. The tension hums, even in digital silence. Caius leans closer to his camera, the blue-tinged reflection of schematics scrolling in his irises.

"That's Brotherhood firmware," he says, his voice low and clipped. "But scrambled—deliberate obfuscation of the protocol handshakes."

Lucien's brow furrows, lips pressed bloodless. "Who's rotated through your staff this week, Orion? Any maintenance contracts, inventory audits…? We've had support crews cross-checking between all sites. Someone could piggyback under almost any pretext."

Darius lifts a hand. "Helios could bribe a staff intermediary. Or—worse—this isn't just Helios. Someone inside. Someone with clearance." His words hang heavy, the implication thick as cordite after a shot.

The siblings of trust—Orion can feel it—are splintering, the familiar cadence of their voices splashed with suspicion. Caius's eyes flick sidelong, not quite meeting Lucien's. Lucien responds in measured syllables, each one chosen with precision. Even Darius, usually steady as granite, watches the corners of the tablet image as if scanning for lies. The Brotherhood, built on shared secrets, now trembles before the possibility that the attack comes from beneath their own roof.

Elara—the only figure in the room with flesh-and-bone weight—sits at the end of the table, her back straight, knuckles pale where they rest atop a legal pad. Orion senses the tangle in his own heart, the ache of having Elara bear witness to this unraveling, when she's spent weeks demanding order among their chaos.

Her voice, when it comes, slices clean through the rising static. "Before you start pointing fingers at shadows, shut everything down," Elara urges. "Audit the local network, comb the feeds. No calls about sensitive matters—no messages, no whispers, not until we control the perimeter. Let paranoia drive us to diligence, not civil war."

Caius blinks, cornered between defensiveness and grudging respect. Darius nods, murmuring something quiet about resilience, but the miasma of doubt doesn't clear—it seethes, unspoken, in wary glances and stifled breaths.

Orion's hands move almost autonomously, flicking through surveillance records on his second device. The week's oddities stack against each other like crooked dominoes: Seraphina fielding cryptic calls she claims not to recall; board members arriving early or lingering late; spikes in Nova's security access logs—granted, revoked, granted again—in sleep-troubled hours.

"They want us suspicious. Splintered. Whoever built this," Orion says, holding up the velvet-lined transmitter, "understands our tech and our blind spots. It's not just a threat—it's an invitation to eat each other alive."

Lucien's voice turns brittle. "When unity breaks, so does our defense. I'll have a sweep started in every Brotherhood residence. We'll need warrants, discretion—media heat is climbing enough as it is."

Caius leans forward, steepling his fingers. "I'll break down the encryption, trace every echo. We find the leak, or we don't survive the fall."

"You still trust your team, Orion?" Darius asks, quietly direct.

Orion doesn't answer at first, just pushes back from the table, his gaze skimming over Elara. In her eyes, he finds not fear, but the tempered shine of resolve—a steadying counterforce in the electric swirl of meetings and accusations. He wonders, for a moment, how long that anchor will hold if the storms keep coming.

He ends the call. The tablet's screen goes dark. A shaker of dread swirls at the pit of his stomach—personal and collective, the sense that this breach is only the start, the scratching of claws on glass before the real break. The fractured cadence of their voices, the narrowed eyes—even among those he'd once have trusted without hesitation—echoes long after the silence smothers the room. The tension will not yield, only coil tighter, the Brotherhood and its orbit tilting steadily toward distrust.

Orion glances across the table at Elara, noting the subtle frown that deepens as the room seems to shrink around them. The study is suddenly too small, the night too keen—a feeling that, from this moment on, everything they do must be doubted, even the simplest gesture, every word whispered, every meal passed hand to hand.

Orion sinks onto the low-slung blue couch, shoulders sagging as though some invisible tide drags him under. Distant thunder rattles glass, and the floor-to-ceiling windows shimmer with city light—a fractured mirror of neon, storms shifting above distant towers. Behind him, the penthouse glows in shards: the kitchen spills faint gold into the living room, wine-dark shadows stretching across polished marble. He stares at the music box—still and silent now at the edge of the coffee table—as if it holds answers he already dreads.

"Elara," he calls, his voice fraying at the edges, pulse quick behind every syllable. A beat lingers. Then her footfalls pad softly across the marble, barely audible above the far-off surge of traffic and rain. She slips into the cold lamp glow beside him, sitting with her hands folded just so, knees angled his way.

For a long moment, silence presses its weight between them. Orion's gaze hovers over the city, then falls to his own hands. He rubs at the scar down his left forearm—an old mark, white and faded, but aching in memory now.

"I keep telling myself we're ahead of them. That every protocol I built will hold." His words twist, resigned, bitter with the taste of old failures. "But it always finds a way in, doesn't it? All this glass and chromed steel... it's nothing but an illusion. The Brotherhood, Nova... us. Someone's already inside the gates."

Elara's eyes soften. She leans in minutely, her voice steady and grounding, a gentle bottom note below the electric hum between them. "The walls aren't what protect us, Orion. And you don't have to carry all of it alone." She draws a slow, deep breath, steadying her own nerves—he tastes the calmness in her voice, crafted as carefully as one of his own algorithms.

"Whatever's coming, we stay ahead of it together. You. Me. Nova. No more secrets. No more lone-wolf saves. We watch each other's backs, even in here. Especially in here."

Orion laughs, a quick, rough sound, but there's gratitude buried in its roughness—a recognition of the lifeline she throws him when he least deserves it. Rain ticks against the glass, soft then staccato, and somewhere in another wing, Nova dreams, fragile and blissfully unaware. For a flicker, he envies that innocence.

"You don't know what it's like," he says, his voice a murmur. "To wonder, every time someone smiles the wrong way or says the right name at the wrong moment, if they're the crack in the foundation. Every time I trust, everything falls apart—and someone gets hurt." His thumb presses hard into the music box's engraved lid. "I can't lose this family again, Elara. Not her. Not you."

She shifts closer, her hand brushing over his knuckles—brief, controlled, as though even warmth must obey her order. "I'm not leaving. Nova's not alone. You start pushing us away, and you'll make their job a hell of a lot easier." Her tone is steely as drawn wire, unsentimental, but underneath, he hears her anxiety too: the fear she'll fall short, that the rules she clings to aren't enough.

He breaks the contact with a sigh and rakes a trembling hand through his hair. On the gleaming glass table, his palm hovers over the music box, then works the casing open with brisk, twitchy precision. He pulls the transmitter's chip from its velvet nest and feeds it into his slim black scanner, its surface cold and slick like river stone after rain. The device pings, lights flickering—a digital heartbeat. On the wall screen, lines of fractured code dance: zeros and ones glinting down like stormwater down a skyscraper's side, stuttering, unresolved.

The scanner emits rapid beeps: timestamped, deliberate, spaced by fractions that suggest intent rather than accident. Orion stiffens, reading patterns where only chaos should be. With a shiver, he watches binary cascade into a brief, jagged sequence—more than a signature, less than a warning. A pulse counting down, its meaning occult but malignant.

He feels the storm in his blood. Old wounds ache, invisible—memories of boardroom betrayals and paparazzi hounding his every mistake, of Nova's mother dying in the cold hush of a hospital room, of secrets cracked open by carelessness or misplaced trust. So many rescued at the last second—so many more that slipped through. This is different, a new kind of siege: smarter, vicious, precise. It is war waged in hidden codes, by someone who understands exactly what will break him.

He rises, boots silent on the stone, and stalks to the window. The skyline is a mingled landscape of hope and menace—bridges arching in pale blue, towers gouging clouds. Lightning threads the distant dark. Orion grips the cold metal frame, forehead leaning into glass, closed eyes reflecting a world always just out of his reach.

A flicker of movement behind insists he's not alone—Elara, upright and unwavering, watching with the poise of a sentry who knows she can't control the weather, only weather the storm. All the while, the city thrums with a thousand secrets and the taste of incoming rain.

He stands motionless, outlined by the trembling lights, his own image doubling back on itself. The room behind him is filled with the proof of all he loves—the echo of a child's laughter, the hum of trust not yet broken, the raw edge of a promise made and barely held. He will not flinch. Not yet.

Pushed Away

Orion doesn't knock—he never does when anger prowls inside him like a captive animal. Instead, the glass doors rattle as he pushes through, his gait clipped and loud, footsteps cracking against the white marble. The penthouse is a broken symphony—storm clouds pressing against the windows, gray light cut into ribbons across the cold floor. Shadows hunker against steel beams. In their center, Elara stands at the built-in bookcase, sorting Nova's pens in color order. She looks up—her stillness is wary.

"You want to explain what I heard?" Orion's voice carves through the silence, raw and unsteady, the question a snarl dragged from somewhere deeper than his chest.

Her hands, steady a heartbeat ago, hover in the air now.

"I met him for Nova," she begins, careful, her tone meant to soothe but stretched thin. "He's a prosecutor. He has influence with the school board. They're pushing for—"

Orion slashes his hand through the air. "Don't," he spits, something flickering behind his eyes—pain sharpened to accusation. "I heard enough. You feeding him information. Whispering about my competency."

Elara doesn't flinch, but her shoulders round defensively. "You're jumping to conclusions. I never said any—"

"You think I don't know what betrayal smells like?" He closes the distance, each syllable brittle. "One leak and the vultures circle Nova again. Board threats, custody hearings—the media's tracking every breath I take. You knew, Elara. You knew what getting cozy with your ex would look like. Or didn't you care?"

Her voice slices through his, calm but undercut with anger. "This is about Nova. I'd never sabotage her stability. Or yours. But you don't even give me a moment to explain before you assume the worst."

"Explain it, then!" Orion's words burst out, too loud, ricocheting through the glass and chrome. Thunder peals somewhere—right overhead or in his bloodstream, he can't tell. "You know how many knives I've already taken this week? Caius warning me about PR landmines, the board whispering about removing me, threats showing up in Nova's backpack. Now this—my supposed anchor running back to someone who'd gut me if it helped his career. Do you think I'm stupid?"

A tremor flashes across Elara's face, but she stands firm, chin raised. "No. I think you're hurt and scared, and making wild leaps because it's easier than actually listening. I told him nothing about you or this house. If you really saw me—if you bothered to trust anyone besides yourself—you'd know that."

He laughs, cold and brittle, pacing away to the window, hands clenching. The world outside boils, the horizon cloaked in iron. Rain lashes at the glass, city lights bleeding in streaks. For a fractured second, Orion sees not Elara, but the ghost of his sister's face, whispering forgiveness he'll never deserve. Everyone leaves; the world takes and takes, and the one time he lets himself believe, cracks appear at the foundations.

He spins, words spilling with an edge that tastes like grief. "It's always the same, isn't it? My mother, my sister, lovers—hell, business partners. It's all smoke and shadows until the rug is yanked out from under me. Now threats are in my own house. In my own family. You said you'd protect Nova. You said you'd stay. How am I supposed to believe it?"

Elara's jaw sets. Her eyes are bright, hurt and fury mingling. "I stay because I choose to. I've kept every promise. I've told you every truth. But if you insist on building walls out of every bad memory, there's nothing I can do for you."

A beat of silence, thick with static and the distant rumble of the storm. Orion's breath shakes. Bitter words pool at the tip of his tongue, and for a moment he fights them—fights the part of him that wants to rewind time, reach for her hand, beg her not to go. But the tidal pull of old wounds is too strong.

"I can't," he says, the fracture audible. "I can't trust you. Not after this. Pack your things." He turns, jaw rigid, every muscle straining. "Leave. Tonight."

The word lingers, ghostly. Elara stands frozen, disbelief carving deep lines into her expression. She doesn't move—almost doesn't breathe—as Orion storms past her, eyes fixed on the floor as if by refusing to look back, he might escape everything unraveling behind him.

The penthouse swallows the last of his footsteps, all sound collapsed to stormlight and Elara's stunned silence.

Elara's suitcase lies open on the guest room bed, its canvas edges gaping like a wound. Pale light from the steel-framed window pools over the scattered memories: her neat row of notebooks, Nova's music box—she leaves that behind—and a faded scarf she's promised never to lose. She moves slowly, as though each item she folds is a confession. Her hands tremble so badly she nearly drops her phone. Only the rhythmic hum of city traffic, just audible through double glass, keeps her tethered to the present.

At the door, Nova's shadow flickers—a slim, silent silhouette. She wears her worry plainly, small shoulders curled inward, dark hair tangled from hours spent hiding in her room while the storm broke overhead. With each careful movement, Elara tells herself to keep breathing. Suitcase, toothbrush, paperback novel, glass case for her glasses. Only essentials. The walls in here once seemed simply unadorned; tonight, they press in with uncanny vacancy.

Elara reaches for a soft blue sweater but halts, sensing Nova's presence behind her.

"Elara?" Nova's voice is no more than a whisper, raw with the kind of fear that is brittle and old. "Are you really leaving?"

Elara swallows the ache. "Just for a little while, sweetheart."

Nova edges closer, eyes wide with pleading hope. "You can't. Please. Orion's always angry, but you—" Her breath catches, uneven, desperation in every word. "You can't just go. If you leave, everything will break."

Elara crouches in the patch of cold light and gathers Nova's trembling hands in hers. "I'm not leaving you," she says, forcing her voice to be gentle, steady—wishing she could believe it's true in the ways a child needs. "Sometimes grown-ups get things wrong. But you haven't done anything wrong, Nova. I... I promise I won't be far."

Nova shakes her head, silent tears sliding down her cheeks. Then, abruptly, she tears her hands free and flees across the living room, her footsteps too soft to break the echoing hush. She stops before the opaque glass of Orion's study door.

"Uncle Orion!" Her cry is muffled, strained by sobs. "You have to fix this! Please! Can you stop—stop fighting?" She presses her forehead against the door, waiting for a miracle, as if her words might melt the iron that's settled in this home.

Silence coils inside the study, pressed tight between glass, paper, and regret.

Beyond the door, Orion is a study in defeat. He sits hunched at his desk, so far forward that his shoulders seem to collapse in on themselves. His hands shield his face. On the surface, he wears his usual armor—straight lines, dark suit, the flicker of blue from a hidden screen. But every ounce of command is gone from his posture, every word shriveled and hidden under a mountain of guilt. He cannot answer. Shame has rendered him voiceless.

Nova's sobs fade, replaced by the quiet pulse of her breathing—thin, quick gasps that speak of too many nights spent alone after slamming doors.

Elara finishes packing in silence. All her defiance has been leached away, drained by the knowledge that she has become part of the chaos she swore to protect Nova from. This is not the story she meant to write for the child. Yet she moves with the slow determination of those who have no choice but to go.

She finds Nova trembling by the foyer, half-hidden by the grand curve of the staircase. The foyer is an architect's dream, wrapped in marble and glass, but tonight it is only a threshold between things that matter and things that must be survived.

"Nova." Elara kneels, holding out her arms. "Come here, love."

Nova runs to her, burying her face in Elara's scarf.

Elara presses her face into Nova's hair, breathing in the scent of childhood—blueberry shampoo, sleep, and the ozone tang of the coming storm. She wants to promise forests in spring and pancakes in the morning, but in this penthouse, wishes are brittle things. Her resignation lodges in her chest. "Listen to me. I'm not leaving forever. I care about you. I'll always care about you, Nova. No storm lasts forever. You believe that for both of us, okay?"

Nova clings tighter. "Promise you'll come back."

Elara's hands shake as she gently unclasps Nova's hold. "I promise," she says, though her voice is a thread. "Be brave. You're not alone."

She draws away, brushing a tear from Nova's cheek. The penthouse feels cavernous and strange, the play of lantern-gray evening across marble turning every shadow into an accusation. Elara should say more—truths, apologies, amends. But the words knot in her throat.

She lingers at the door, suitcase in hand, watching Nova, who stands fragile and adrift under the high-vaulted ceiling. The foyer's glass reflects both their faces—one wavering, one determined, both uncertain.

Elara exhales, then slips into the hallway, leaving the penthouse breathless and dim. The door's final click is soft, but it echoes for a long time after, reverberating down the corridor while Nova stands, tears painting bright streaks over her quiet courage.

Orion sits motionless behind his glass-topped desk, a silver-blue glow spilling from the phone beside his wrist. Every sharp surface of the penthouse reflects that icy light—city windows frosted with condensation, marble floors catching uneasy shadows. He does not answer when Caius's name flashes again, just silences it with a thumb jerked in irritation, his jaw tense against the pressure building at his temples. The screen shifts: a new notification, encrypted, with a flickering message pulsing just beneath the surface—"Watch the shadows in your own house."

He stares until the symbols dance, his spine prickling. The penthouse is too quiet now: the silence after a slammed door, the hush of distant traffic beneath thick glass, a storm wind pushing rain against the panes so it sounds like fingers scratching to get in.

His mind circles, wild and aimless: Elara's eyes vivid with pain, Nova's wilted plea as she'd watched Elara leave, the echo of his own voice—too harsh, too frightened—shouting her out. Guilt stirs, sour and insistent beneath all the reasons he'd tried, badly, to build this sanctuary in the sky. Somewhere beneath the stone surface he wears for the world, Orion's pulse thuds with the old terror that everything he loves will shatter, and it will be his fault. He cannot separate Elara's possible betrayal from the thrum of threat beneath his floorboards, the knowledge that cracks in the walls bring invaders—sometimes disguised as trusted allies.

Messages like the one on his screen have come before, but never with this chill, this sense of someone watching and waiting for him to crumble. Once, the Brotherhood had been untouchable—code, power, allies everywhere. Now even his home feels perforated and fragile, every argument a breach for danger to slip through. Orion wonders, not for the first time, if this is how empires fall: slow, from within, rotting before the storm even hits.

Upstairs, Nova lies curled on her side atop a tangle of pale sheets. The soft gleam from her terrarium glimmers through streaked glass, throwing shifting shapes across her walls. She draws Elara's blue scarf tighter under her chin, the faint scent of lavender and chalk dust clinging to the threads. Her breath is shallow and uneven, tears staining her cheeks, her chest tight with the dread that Elara's absence brings on dark nights. The distant rumble of thunder rattles the window sash, and Nova buries her face, wishing silently that the storm would sweep them all away so she could start again, in a world without sharp words or slammed doors or empty spaces at bedtime.

Across the city, Elara perches on the edge of a nondescript sofa. The apartment is mostly a box, pale walls marked only by the halo of lamplight and the shimmer of rain beading on glass. She hasn't changed out of her work clothes, nor bothered to unpack. Her hand trembles as she dials Lila, her voice raw but careful as she speaks.

"Lila. Please—check in on Nova tomorrow. She's probably scared. Just…I couldn't go back. Not tonight." Elara's fingers press the bridge of her nose, holding back another wave of tears. Silence swells in the gap between her and the rest of her world.

"It's not your fault, Elara, you know that?" Lila's voice is balm, but it can't reach deep enough tonight.

Elara lets the words hang in the rain-muted dark. She watches the city outside—towering silhouettes shrouded in weather, neon cutting through the haze—and wonders if the scars carved tonight are permanent. Her phone sits cooling beside her, dark except for the faint afterimage of Nova's smiling lock screen, a tiny universe slipping further from her grasp.

Down below, in the slick-black street, a figure stands beneath a flickering lamp post, coat drawn high against the wind. Rain peppers the pavement and blurs the tower lights into wavering constellations on the slick asphalt. The stranger remains still, gaze fixed upward. To anyone passing, just another silhouette in the storm's embrace, but their intent is a needle: precise, patient, and aimed at the windows five stories above, where the living room still glows faintly, blue and empty.

Inside, every ticking second presses the fracture—Orion hunched in his private office, ignoring the Brotherhood's lifeline in favor of icy paranoia. Nova, silent and adrift, small against the storm in a kingdom built for protection but echoing with abandonment. Elara, talking in whispers to the only friend she dares trust, crossing another imaginary distance with every beat of the rain. And outside, the city hums with restless energy, as if sensing blood in the water. Vulnerability inside feeds audacity outside; as trust unravels in the high tower, enemies at the gate scent their coming opportunity. Only the wind bears witness, coiling around the glass and steel—a tightening pressure, the promise that every storm, on the inside or out, is only beginning.

Broken Bonds

The hush inside Orion Vega's penthouse is nearly as sharp as the city's encroaching twilight. Glass walls reflect the skyline's glitter, casting fractured webs of neon blue over the steel-and-marble landscape of his living room. Footsteps echo quietly, dulled by the soft carpets and the thick air. Orion paces behind the couch, phone in hand, thumb flicking too fast through encrypted messages, unread headlines, and a storm of boardroom threats. Each time Elara's quiet footsteps cross into his periphery, he reroutes his attention—phone up, jaw set, expression carved in glass.

"Nova's spelling folder is in the kitchen if she wants help," Elara says, her voice clipped but courteous as she stands near the kitchen threshold. Her posture is deliberate, as though she's inserting herself into a circuit Orion keeps trying to close. Light from the recessed strips splays over her hair, turning the strands a metallic black.

Orion responds without lifting his eyes from the screen. "I've got it handled," he mutters, the words cool enough to fog the air, and he moves, quick and silent, edging toward the corridor that leads to his private office. He does not meet her gaze. The chrome handle bites into his palm as he wrestles with the urge to slam the door behind him.

At the coffee table, Nova sits cross-legged on the rug, her tablet black and dormant beneath twitching fingers. The silence here is different from the boardroom—it's full of things unsaid, every word bitten and left to rot. Nova's shoulders round defensively, the thin fabric of her T-shirt bunching as she draws patterns only she can see.

Elara bends, passing Nova a gentle smile; the air smells faintly of citrus from some long-finished glass of water, cool but tinged with unease. "Would you like a little help with those sentences?" Elara's tone softens, directed not at Orion this time but at the small, aching shape on the floor.

Nova looks up, mouth quivering. "Why is everyone so quiet tonight?" Her question isn't loud, but it cleaves through the room like a cold knife. Orion stops moving. His knuckles whiten on his phone. Elara straightens without a word, her face composed but the fabric at her elbow tense where her hand curls tight. The silence is raw, scraping. Orion feels it vibrate in his teeth, behind his temples.

He stares at the glow outside—city lights flickering alive, each window a puzzle box he can't solve. The skyline is both a fortification and a prison. He can hear the hum of the refrigerator in the open-plan kitchen, the distant rattle of car horns several stories below. Everything inside feels smaller, compressed, the penthouse suddenly more glass cage than haven. In the reflection, Elara's figure hovers behind him, her form fractured by the beveled edge of glass.

Dinner is a ballet of avoidance and ritual. They take their places around the angular glass table, a trio adrift. Nova is first, her legs swinging, napkin twisted in her lap. The overhead light casts shadowed crescents beneath her eyes, making her appear even smaller. Orion stabs at a roasted carrot with unnecessary force; the tines scrape across porcelain, the sound grating. The steam from the food—savory, almost earthy—slips unnoticed into the currents of their discomfort.

Elara tries. "Nova, did you finish that story about the fox in the city? Was it a happy ending?" Her tone is light, offering a rope across the chasm. Nova lifts her eyes hopefully, but Orion's voice slices across the space, not answering, just nudging the salt toward Nova with a brusque, "Pass it here, kiddo."

Nova pinches a breadcrumb between her thumb and forefinger, as if it's a secret. "The fox got lost," she murmurs, eyes flicking from Elara to Orion, uncertainty blooming in her shoulders. Orion hears the note of distress, but everything inside him is tangled: guilt for failing to protect Nova's peace, suspicion tightening his chest whenever Elara edges too close. If he admits she's good for Nova, isn't that another authority ceded—another brick out of the wall he's built since his sister's death?

Elara breathes long and slow, shoulders squared. She looks at Orion just once, silence a question between them, but he will not meet it.

The table is set for three but feels like an interrogation: every utensil laid with surgical precision, every word a turn in a trial with no verdict. Orion answers only when Nova speaks, never volunteering, never opening. He registers Elara's efforts at conversation, her attempts to draw Nova's laughter back, but keeps his replies perfunctory and flat. Each pause stretches, growing heavier than the dusk pressing at the windows.

Finally, Nova finishes her meal first. She stands, the legs of her chair scraping softly, a hesitant hover before she gathers her plate. Nobody stops her as she slips from the table, feet whispering toward her room.

Orion and Elara are left at opposite ends of the shadowed dining space, the city's fractured light shimmering around them, neither daring to speak, motionless in their quiet stalemate.

Nova's room hovers on the edge of silence and storm—a world painted in blurred lavender shadows and the drowsy, uncertain glow of constellations scattered overhead. Moonlight slants through linen curtains, making the soft pastel walls waver, as if the quiet itself presses inward, closing the air tight. Nova curls on her side atop the tangled bedsheet, knees drawn to her chest, arms locked tightly, clutching the thin cotton of her nightshirt over her rapidly fluttering heart. Her breaths are short, clipped, delivered in small desperate gasps that fog the air beneath her chin.

A faint, trembling voice slices the hush, barely more than a whisper. "Elara?" Her fingers curl until her knuckles whiten. Each exhale feels like running out of air underwater, the weight of silence growing, crowding out thought. The plush stars glued above—the only guardians she truly trusts—blur and multiply. They seem impossibly far away.

Elara enters with brisk steps, the door slipping closed behind her, slicing away the larger darkness of the penthouse beyond. The shift in air, sharp and cool, is threaded with lavender vapor from Nova's diffuser. Elara goes straight to the bedside, lowering herself onto her knees so quickly the movement barely registers as a sound.

"Nova, honey, breathe with me." Her voice is measured, lower than normal, soothing but cut with command. She gathers Nova's chilled hands—smaller than the palm of her own—and rubs slow circles over trembling knuckles. The girl's whole body quivers like a small animal beneath a predator's stare.

With her own pulse pounding at her throat, Elara counts a rhythm—inhale, hold, exhale, counting four, then six, then eight—letting the numbers anchor her as much as the child. Her mind slams shut doors to earlier arguments and Orion's cold retreat, to her private sense of betrayal. Focus. Only Nova exists now: the panic, the shuddering breath, the small fingers clutching at frayed cotton as if gripping the edge of a precipice.

Elara's movements are precise as ritual, a choreography stitched by years comforting children through storms of the mind. She reaches for the weighted plush owl at the foot of the bed—a talisman in moments like this, its softness dense and grounding—and nudges Nova's hands open, patient as the tide smoothing jagged stones. "Let's hold Ollie, hmm?" Her words are gentle, the syllables stretched and muffled by the hush. She tucks the plush into Nova's lap, curling Nova's arms around the heavy form. Small fingers twitch.

Nova sucks in a ragged breath, but tears spill down her cheeks, warm and salt-sticky.

The door bursts open. Orion freezes at the threshold, shadowed against the lamp's meager light. His expression is unreadable, jaw clamped so tight that his cheekbones stand out like cut glass; fists bunch at his sides, sleeves rumpled at the cuffs. He says nothing, only drinks in the sight—Elara's head bent close to Nova's, the trembling of the child who is both his blood and his greatest failing. In the hush, Elara feels his turmoil ripple across the room. She doesn't look up. She can't risk breaking the fragile spell. Instead, she smooths sweaty curls from Nova's forehead and draws a slow breath.

"Let's count the stars, sweet pea." Elara nods up, eyes guiding Nova's gaze to the familiar cartoon constellations scattered above the bed, faintly aglow. "Start with Orion's Belt, right there. One, two, three." Her own tone is calm but loaded, a lifeline thrown across writhing water. "Just breathe with the stars. Let them fill your lungs for you."

Nova's body jerks, then stills. Her gaze follows Elara's finger, finding tiny blue dots. "One, two, three..." The numbers come out as a whisper, thin as mist, but the rhythm of her breaths begins to change—slower, deeper, not perfect but enough. Elara keeps her hand steady, voice a reassuring murmur, building a lattice between panic and calm. Each star becomes an anchor. Eight stars... ten... Nova's breathing knits into a more regular pattern. Fatigue drapes her muscles, and finally she sags into Elara's side, the plush owl squeezed against her chest, a shuddering sigh leaving her lips.

Orion stands motionless, the lines in his face haunted. He looks like a man banished behind glass, acutely aware of every inch separating him from the bed. Elara, feeling dew-slick hair beneath her palm, gathers Nova against her, rocking ever so slightly. She doesn't look at Orion but senses the way the room's tension pivots—ice splintering into something rawer, closer to surrender.

Tear tracks run down Nova's face, soaking into Elara's sleeve; sweat beads along her hairline, the room thick with the sour tang of adrenaline and the faint perfume of lavender. There's no room for Elara's personal ache—no space for doubt or for the jagged wound Orion's earlier words left. Here, she is refuge and ritual, her own pulse steady and strong because that's what Nova's world requires. Stone beneath the storm, because she must be.

In another life, Elara learned to be that steady ground, in rooms like this—different patterns, desperate voices—and every scar along her heart has taught her exactly how to breathe enough strength into panic to keep a child safe a little longer. Her role is clear now: not just tutor, not just employee—protector. The lines of family and duty blur in the hush. She grounds herself in the child's simple weight, letting the world narrow down to the pattern of breathing and the warmth of trust in Nova's slackening grip.

For just this moment, thunder and betrayal are far away.

The hallway is quiet, save for the fading echo of Nova's choked breaths behind the closed door. Muted lamplight leaks out in a broken wedge, painting dusty gold over the polished hardwood and onto Orion's bare feet. He leans his weight against the wall beneath a modern abstract canvas, letting the cold plaster press through his shirt as he draws in an unsteady breath. His phone hangs forgotten in his hand. He stares at the vague reflection gleaming in the blackened screen, the features that match his sister's—Nova's mother—now cast hollow and wary.

Elara closes Nova's door gently, her touch precise enough to quiet the click of the latch. She stands with her back to the wood for a beat, letting her head tip forward, shoulders tense under the soft glow from the child's nightlight. Her hands curl in toward her chest, missile-tight, knuckles drained of color. Every line of her is exhaustion and control, the kind that comes only at the price of burning through all the reserves of the day.

Orion finds his voice first, though gravel coats it. "How did you know what to do?" The words come out before he can temper them, softer than the harsh bark he usually wields as armor. He steps forward, slow, as if approaching some wild and wounded thing.

Elara doesn't straighten, doesn't let her arms drop. "Darius," she says, tone a steady current running beneath fatigue. "He showed me some techniques. For episodes like this." Her eyes flicker, catching the light and returning something determined beneath it. "That's all I care about, giving her—" She breaks off, then starts again, slower. "Giving Nova a shore to hold on to. Even if the rest of us are... not."

A silence settles, thick as storm clouds before midnight rain. Orion rubs a hand over the scar on his forearm, the old burn from a reckless night. He avoids her gaze, blinking hard as if sight alone could keep him in control. Each breath scrapes through his throat: the air here still holds the scent of Nova's soap and the anxious, sharp tang of sweat, mingled with the penthouse's usual ozone coolness and faint, expensive polish.

He tries to keep his voice even. "Thank you, Elara," he says. Simple words. Alien on his tongue, heavy with things he never learned to say—not to lovers, not to colleagues, not to family. His gaze roams over the slick marble and steel and glass of the world he's built, all designed for invincibility. None of it means a thing if Nova is small and afraid behind the door, if the people he lets close keep disappearing anyway.

The chasm inside yawns, old and familiar. Since his sister died—since he took on the child who looks at him with those haunted eyes—every connection feels booby-trapped. Trust becomes a hand hovering uncertainly over a detonator. No matter how careful, everything slips through his grasp.

He swallows, voice fraying at the edges. "I keep thinking... everyone I trust, everyone Nova cares about, they leave. In the end. What if it happens again?" Orion glances up once, fast, as if the question itself might bite. His eyes are too bright beneath the angled light; he blinks, jaw tight, then shakes his head.

For a fragile instant, they simply stand. Elara lowers her arms, uncrossing them with the grace of a drawn breath. "Nova isn't alone," she says, quiet but unwavering. "Not while I'm here. I'm not leaving her just because things get... complicated between adults." She meets his gaze directly—a challenge and a kindness mingled in one level look. "You don't have to trust me. But she does. That's what matters most."

Orion's mouth works, searching for a retort, an accusation, some scrap of old stubbornness to hide behind. But nothing settles. The tension between them shimmers, an invisible thread stretched taut—anchoring, maybe, instead of threatening to snap.

Outside, the city spills neon and shadow across the windows. The distant sound of horns and life below is muffled, rendered small by the glass fortress wrapped around them. In this hallway cocooned in dim light, the usual pulse of power and chaos has retreated, replaced by the hush after a crisis, the scent of lavender drifting from Nova's room mingling with the metallic clean of the penthouse.

There is no blame in Elara's stance, only weary assurance. And for a moment, Orion lets himself believe in the possibility of not being abandoned. The ache barely dulls. He holds himself still, as if movement might break the fragile peace settling in the half-lit corridor.

They remain in silence, the soft illumination from beneath Nova's door casting them as half-shadows on the wall. The city's blue glow pushes against encroaching darkness, and between the two adults, something flickers—a first, quiet understanding fighting to take root amid the wreckage.

Low city thunder flickers behind the glass, tracing fault lines across the steel-and-indigo hush of the living room. The penthouse feels halfway between evening and night—a blue world suspended over the pulse of the city, the hum of traffic sealed outside by glass walls. Soft pools of lamplight slide across marble and chrome, but leave the corners shadowed, uncertain. Elara leads Orion forward, unhurried, each step a careful negotiation over broken ground.

She stops just shy of the rug, turning so the soft halo settles on her hair and the hard lines of exhaustion soften on her face. Her voice, steady but quiet, parts the hush. "I'm staying, Orion. For Nova. That hasn't changed, even if everything else feels like it has." Her hand hesitates, then brushes his skin—warm, trembling, honest. The touch lingers, barely there, like an apology no one says aloud.

Orion stands still, head inclined, jaw tense as if every word is barricaded behind his teeth. He lets the silence stretch, searching for something in Elara's features—relief, anger, hope, maybe all of them. He gives a single nod, haunted eyes fixed on the hand that almost reaches for his. Part of him wants to break, to reach back and erase the scar of mistrust; another part fears one word will shatter the fragile equilibrium, send her slipping away for good.

The moment suspends. Light flickers on his knuckles as he flexes his hands, not knowing if they'll be fists or a gesture of surrender.

From down the corridor, small bare feet pad softly across stone. Nova appears at the threshold in faded pajamas, sleep-mussed hair haloed by lamplight. She carries no sound but her breathing—quick, careful, as though she's moving through some delicate, invisible web. She crosses the living room and stands between them, gaze searching both faces with gravity beyond her years. She reaches out, slipping one hand into Elara's and the other up to Orion's callused palm, threading herself between apprehension and hope.

Elara's fingers squeeze gently. Orion looks down at Nova's hand in his, glove-soft and trembling. He feels its warmth—pulse, frailty, innocence clutching him to this world, this consequence. Nova looks up, her eyes wide, the storm of earlier panic dulled but not dispersed. Her presence bridges the gap but asks silent, impossible questions: will you stay? will you fight for us?

Without thinking, Orion's thumb smoothes Nova's knuckles. An ache coils behind his ribs. He senses how much they all need this moment—this illusion of unity, battered but unbroken.

His phone vibrates, cutting through the hush. On the glass tables, the sound is a ripple through water. Orion drags his gaze away from Nova, retrieving the device from his pocket. The screen lights his face with a cold, digital glow: a new encrypted message, cycling symbols until the words resolve. "Shadows move closer. Guard what you love, even from within." His thumb presses the display, knuckles whitening. The implication pulses beneath the surface—danger not just outside, but within their walls, their defenses, their very hearts.

A tremor runs through the back of Orion's mind. Shadows—what does it mean? Is it Caius's warning, that the Brotherhood's circle is closing tighter, hiding rot? Is Helios's long reach already here, poisoning the air in these rooms? He wonders which is more corrosive: the threat from faceless enemies or the doubt that's grown between him and those he'd give everything to protect. Nova's hand is small, trusting, utterly exposed.

The possibility of betrayal—internal, insidious—blooms in his mind. In a world of secret codes and enemies behind glass towers, perhaps the greatest danger is what lingers in the places you once thought safe. Elara says she is staying, but trust feels like walking out into a storm with nowhere to hide. Was this how it was always meant to go? Did the archive countdown start in their own living room instead of some distant server room, a fracture that broke first at the kitchen table?

He desperately wants to believe that unity is possible again, that storms can wash clean rather than destroy. Yet reconciliation, like the city's stubborn lights against the dusk, holds itself out always just beyond his reach. The shapes of Elara and Nova beside him should anchor him, but a part of him calculates loss, almost expects it. If the message is true, if the shadows move closer, will he have the courage to close ranks against the world—or will he lose both of them to the darkness within his own walls?

They stand together, skin lit by the blue pulse of city twilight. Orion's hand tightens involuntarily around Nova's, the cryptic message blazing in the periphery of his vision. Elara's warmth lingers at his side, uncertain but real, while Nova's fingers bridge the chasm between hope and the deep, encroaching shadows pressing against the penthouse glass.

Heartfelt Reunion

Orion's private study is a chamber carved above the pulse of the city, perched just behind glass that holds back the storm of night. Outside, skyscrapers scrawl neon sigils across indigo skies, the world below silent and aloof. In here, the air is velvet-thick with the metallic tang of old books, a hint of leather, and Orion's own breath hovering jagged between his ribs. He sits hunched, dwarfed by the broad-armed chair, wrapped in shadows tinged a midnight blue from the city haze. The only bright thing is the photograph caught in his hand—its edges frayed, silver frame worn smooth where his thumb presses, again and again.

The photograph, as it has a hundred times before, opens a wound. His sister's eyes hold a constellation of laughter, her head tilted with careless joy. In her arms, infant Nova squints at the world with a curiosity that, in hindsight, feels cruel in its innocence. Orion's thumb finds the outline of his sister's smile. He traces it while, beneath his skin, memory becomes a gravity, hot and leaden. For a moment, breath deserts him. He remembers the day the photo was taken—the warm, milk-sweet scent of Nova's skin, the chaos of a family kitchen, the taste of cinnamon on toast, laughter tripping over itself between his mother and sister, the window cracked open to let in sun and sirens.

But the past is never soft with him. It lands like a blow. The hollow behind Orion's sternum, carved deeper by every public mistake, every headline that turned his grief into spectacle, aches anew. He wonders if, had he been different, his sister would still be alive. If he hadn't been so obsessed with the next deal, the next rush, the next edge. Guilt collects beneath his tongue, bitter as old coffee. What remains now is obligation—twined tightly with the fear that, at any instant, he'll fail the only person who matters.

He tries, for a moment, to control it. To compartmentalize—he's mastered this survival tactic: categorize, box up, lock away. But tonight the boxes splinter. Images from that morning flicker behind his eyelids—Elara in the kitchen, firm and gentle, coaxing Nova back to herself with a steady hand and that unyielding calm. Nova's panic had sent Orion scrambling inside, helpless as a ghost, feet planted as if he were rooted to the marble tile. Shame nipped at him every time; he, the so-called innovator, could solve a million technical problems but couldn't cross a few feet to soothe a terrified child. Elara's voice—measured, unshaken—was the only bridge. He saw Nova's fists unclench, her breath returning in small, staggered sips because of Elara, not him.

His jaw tightens. The city outside is beautiful and poisonous; its promise gleams, but never quite enough to fill the ache of absence.

A vibration trembles across the desk—an electronic pulse. Orion's phone glows, the light yellow against cold steel. He leans forward, neck stiff as he unlocks the screen. Only one new message waits. The content is simple, a string of letters whose meaning weighs a thousand times what it should.

Good night, Daddy. I love you.

The word hits him. Daddy. Nova hardly ever used it, cautious, testing the edges of that title as if it might crumble under her tongue. The warmth of it pools in Orion's chest and then, predictably, twists into panic. He tastes salt as he inhales, sees images of Nova slipping away—board members with greasy smiles, social workers with diamond-cut rules, tabloids flashing her face in the same breathless way they'd done to his sister.

He wants to shield Nova from everything. But protection has a cost, and his own craving for control—his refusal to let anyone close—only sharpens the blade of loneliness. Orion wonders if he's already begun to lose her, not to the courts or the vultures, but to his own absence, his own fear to lean in rather than watch from outside the ring of light Elara makes.

He presses the heels of his hands to his eyes, scrubbing away the sting. That old, corrosive urge to retreat claws at him: get up, pour another drink, busy his mind with figures and forecasts until morning. But the photograph—smiling, forgiving, relentless—sits heavy on his thigh. What's left if not to try again?

He rises. The chair's leather groans in protest; the sound is a soft accusation. Orion returns the photograph to its frame, setting it gently on the corner of his desk. The city beyond the windows blinks, indifferent and eternal. He squares his shoulders, forcing his fists to unclench. This time, he won't run from the raw, bleeding center of things. He will find Elara and speak the truth that's curdling in his chest.

He steps into the hall, the hush following him, and leaves the door open behind him as the city's blue light caresses the abandoned study.

Orion pauses at the threshold, half-shadowed by the soft, golden pools of lamplight that spill across the penthouse's family room. The city's distant pulse glimmers behind the windows, cold and unreachable. Against this tapestry, Elara sits cross-legged on the wide navy couch, the pale throw wrapped around Nova's small body clinging to the lines of comfort and exhaustion. Nova's hair fans over the armrest, glinting brown in the muted light. Elara's hand moves slowly, threading through those tangles, her gaze focused somewhere distant—her own silence heavy. Nova's breaths come in quiet, steady waves, rising and falling with the slow tide of sleep.

Orion steps forward. The wool of the carpet hushes his movement, but the air thickens all the same. Elara looks up, eyes hooded but alert. Her fingers pause in Nova's hair, then resume with deliberate gentleness. Orion's chest tightens, the old ache swirling together with everything he's not said. He stops just short of the coffee table—close enough to feel the heat of Elara's presence, far enough that crossing the rest of the gulf feels impossible.

He cannot shake the memory of this morning: Elara in this very room, coaxing Nova's panic into something manageable, every word a lifeline Orion hadn't known how to cast. He'd watched as if from behind glass, powerless, shame burning hot and silent behind his ribs. Now, under the forgiving hush of night, he tries to find something to say that will not shatter this fragile peace.

His voice breaks the stillness, raw. "I'm afraid you'll leave us. Like everyone else."

For a heartbeat, the city seems to hush in sympathy. Elara's shoulders, tense and guarded, loosen. She studies him—not with judgment, but searching, as if weighing the truth of his words against the person she's come to know.

She draws her legs beneath her, turning to face him fully. "You think I haven't thought about running?" Her tone is softer than he expects, the words stripped of accusation. "I'm afraid, too. Of failing Nova. Of not being enough to hold this together. But I made a choice, Orion. I'm here." She glances down at Nova, her thumb tracing slow circles around the child's ear. "I choose to fight for this family. Even when it doesn't make sense. Especially then."

Orion folds in on himself, lowering to the edge of the opposite couch cushion. He presses his knuckles to his lips, staring at the floor's subtle veining. The city lights splay across the marble, fractured and shifting, refusing to stay still. His mind turns with equal volatility—every instinct urging him to build walls, to laugh this off, to return to chaos. But Nova's gentle breathing is an anchor, impossibly delicate and impossibly strong.

Their words teeter between them, uncertain but genuine.

"You know I was never... supposed to be anyone's guardian." He keeps his gaze on Nova, afraid to look at Elara too long. "Every boardroom, every scandal—I could handle all of it. But this—" His throat closes. "I lose everything I try to keep. My sister. My sense. I keep thinking if I let myself hope, it'll all vanish."

Elara leans in, her shadows merging with his. "It's easier to expect the worst. Safer. But Nova doesn't need perfect. She needs people who don't quit on her. Even if they're scared out of their minds."

He dares a glance at her—there is no mockery, only a frank courage he envies. For a moment, he sees her not as an adversary or employee, but as another soul carrying too much, refusing to turn away from a child who trusts too easily.

"Do you hate me?" he asks, the question unvarnished. "For all of it—the chaos, the lies, the way I keep you locked out?"

She shakes her head, lips twitching in the flickering lamplight. "Sometimes I want to. You make it so easy." Her laugh is a low, wry thing, a dam breaking. "But if I hated you, I wouldn't stay. You're trying. That's enough—for now."

He looks at his hands, suddenly aware of how restless they've always been, how they blur from invention to destruction. "I want to do better. For Nova. For us. If you'll let me."

Elara's answer is quiet, certain. "I want that, too."

Across the table, Elara reaches out. Her palm settles over Orion's, cool and steady. He turns his hand, enfolding hers. On the couch, Nova's breathing steadies into the warm rhythm of trust—each breath a fragile promise that perhaps, finally, none of them have to weather the storm alone.

They linger, hands joined, the hush of the city folding around them. Within that shared, uncertain silence, something shifts—fragmented trust beginning to knit itself, thread by trembling thread.

Orion holds Elara's hand, his thumb brushing the slim ridge of her knuckles. He meets her gaze in the hush, the city's glow a blurred mosaic behind the tall windows. His smile comes slowly—a small, careful thing, tentative in birth, like a shaft of light breaking an endless dusk. Forgiveness, and something strange. Relief, maybe, laced with exhaustion. She squeezes back, not with certainty, but hope. His hand is warm, hers unwavering.

He isn't sure how to release the ache inside his throat, so he offers this: a squeeze, a half-formed promise. The silence shivers, fragile.

Elara rises. Her motion is measured—a schoolteacher's calm, but softened at the edges now. She releases his hand and bends toward

Nova, who is curled beneath the weight of a knit blanket, lashes fluttering on flushed cheeks. Elara slides an arm beneath the girl, careful not to disturb the cocoon of comfort, and lifts Nova from the couch. The child stirs, emitting a murmur half lost in sleep. Elara gathers her with practiced gentleness and settles Nova into Orion's lap, then remains beside him—one hand finding his shoulder, steady and sure.

He can feel the press of her palm through the fabric of his shirt, grounding him as surely as gravity. Nova's head fits against his chest, light as a breath's dusk. For a brief moment, the old, raw fear claws at his ribs—he's not sure he deserves the touch or the trust, and yet it anchors him.

Nova blinks. Her brown eyes, still blurred with dreams, fix on Orion. Hesitant, she studies his face—searching for signs of fracture, perhaps, or for the brittle wall that sometimes bars him from her. She finds only softness there. Relief brightens her expression; she beams, the transformation so sudden it nearly undoes Orion. She buries her cheek against his chest, her small palm curling in his sleeve. Her breathing grows quiet again, rhythmic and trusting.

The night outside surges and settles. City lights splinter across the marble floor, casting the living room in hues of ultramarine and molten gold. Orion, Elara, and Nova gather close, knees brushing, arms drawn in, tentative at first. Orion catches Elara's eye—unmasked now, her brows slightly knit not with worry, but vulnerability.

He exhales. The words taste foreign at first, but they grow easier as the hush thickens around them. "I want to be here. With you. With Nova," he says, his voice low. "I promise. I'll be present. Honest. I won't... I won't run anymore." The declarations tumble between them, neither grand nor blustered—only true, born of storms and silence.

They remain together, hands entwined atop Nova's sleeping form, parchment-soft hair draped over Orion's arm. Elara rests her head against Orion's shoulder, her sigh a pale brush of warmth. Nova's hand remains wrapped in his sleeve, an anchor to a present that is suddenly possible. The three of them—so often scattered by fear, regret, and pride—are fused, if only for this moment, into something whole.

Earlier, the penthouse was all edges and cold gloss: steel counters, glass banisters glinting under the city's fierce light. Now, it shrinks to a single island adrift in midnight: the couch, the lamp's muted ring, the hush of their breath. The old symbols of chaos—the implication of endless rooms and relentless newsfeeds, the city's siren call—exist now only beyond the glass. In this fragment of time, all Orion's hungers—his terror, his longing for forgiveness—collapse into a single, pulsing need: to hold what's left, to be what's needed.

He remembers how Elara's steadiness broke the rhythm of panic in Nova's cries earlier, how her sharpness had once grated on him, yet how it steadied him now. He is struck by how crisis, grief's tempest, forces an opening—for love, for frailty, for a promise that feels less like a noose and more like a thread to lead him home.

His mind scours back through jagged nights spent gripping old photographs, hollowed by loss and bitterness. But tonight, as Nova tucks closer, as Elara's touch lingers and forgives, those wounds knit a fraction tighter. The future presses uncertain against the glass panes, sure as thunder teasing the rim of the skyline. That threat remains, always. But for now, he finds himself not alone in the storm. Their silence becomes their refuge, and hope, strange and bright, breathes in the space between their held hands.

The city pulses outside; inside, the world contracts to three figures, bound in collective quiet—a family delicately sewn together. Orion, for once, does not look for an exit.

He only closes his eyes and listens for Nova's tiny breaths and Elara's heartbeat beside his own.

Commitment Tested

A low amber glow spills across the polished surface of the Brotherhood's boardroom table, illuminating only the tense set of Caius Drake's jaw and the hard glint in Lucien Blackwell's eyes as the last man enters. The walls, thick and soundproof, deaden the constant urban pulse outside, swallowing every distant siren and muted horn. Frosted windows throw jagged, ghostlike patterns over Darius Hale's broad silhouette as two other seasoned Brotherhood members close ranks around the oval table. The hiss of the magnetic door lock punctuates the shift from city to sanctum; inside these walls, secrets won't escape—and neither can the men who bear them.

There's an unspoken ritual: hands out of pockets, sleeves rolled up just enough, eyes flicking from screen to screen. Caius lifts his hand, quelling the undercurrent of anxious muttering. His words slice cleanly through the hush—the media campaign against Orion is approaching critical mass. Negative headlines multiply like metastasizing cells: billionaire's recklessness, threat to guardianship, insinuations about family stability. Every network, every feed, seems primed for the fall. The trial looms just beyond the horizon, and with each new leak, the odds twist tighter.

Lucien, razor-sharp in a charcoal suit, flips through his folder. Documents fan out, each page layered with annotated dread: custody statutes, hostile witness lists, surveillance transcripts riddled with redacted lines. His tone is low and methodical—he'll take point in court, guiding arguments like a conductor's baton. Darius looks up from his notes, nodding gravely—he will oversee the securing of Orion's residence, route reconnaissance, and close protection for Nova, lockdown procedures. Caius doesn't flinch from his self-appointed burden: direct PR counterstrike, deploying his own cadre of analysts to stem the bleeding in public perception.

"There is no margin for error," Caius states. His finger taps out a near-silent rhythm on the glass table. "Every frame, every word in the press, is a blade meant to cut us off from each other. They want us to fracture. We don't fracture."

Lucien meets his gaze. "Then we stand as one. If the prosecution goes for the kill, they'll find our shield impenetrable."

Darius's voice has a deeper gravity. "I've doubled watchers at Orion's building. The elevators, the lobby feeds, the stairwell—clean. We rotate codes tonight and tomorrow. Nobody gets close unless we let them."

A slow, collective breath fills the space as strategy unspools in practiced shorthand. The Brotherhood's hidden influence pulses through every sector: judiciaries that can be tipped, editors bribed or defanged, corporate rivals quietly reminded of old debts. Their reputation is less a rumor than folklore—a constellation of invisible hands manipulating outcomes for the greater good. Under the city's glitter and grime, they are the vigilant keepers of an order that no one acknowledges, but everyone depends on when crisis strikes too close to home.

Caius unlocks his encrypted tablet, the thin digital hum filling the room with promise and tension. Fingers flying, he composes a message—short, ciphers disguising even pronouns and names. Delivered in seconds to Orion and Elara, its meaning is elemental: stand firm; we shield you whatever comes. There's power in code, in silence, in refusing to give their adversaries a single tell or leak.

"PR's already on standby. If they push another scandal tonight, I'll have counter-footage and expert denials live in twenty minutes," Caius promises quietly.

Lucien allows himself a wry half-smile. "You're always three steps ahead."

"I prefer to keep it at least four," Caius murmurs, but apprehension needles just beneath his smile. He knows the machinery of patrician power doesn't always run smoothly; even he's carried the scars of trust misplaced, arrangements betrayed. Still, he cannot yield or waver in the face of this storm. The city depends on men like him to absorb punishment—he, and the Brotherhood, are the ballast beneath everyone else's calm.

Darius's steady eyes linger on Caius, and then Lucien. Resolve flows in silence. Without a word, all five men rise and gather around the table. Palms rest atop cool glass, knuckles tense, a tacit bond forming a living circuit. For a moment, the chamber holds its breath: this is what loyalty tastes like—metallic and electric at the back of the tongue, settling in the space between bones.

Chairs scrape softly. Their silhouettes peel away, drifting toward the blacked-out door and the uncertain dark that waits beyond these walls, each man already reaching for encrypted comms and unlocked safes, weapons and documents arranged like votive offerings for the coming conflict.

Caius lets the last of them pass. He flicks the lights off: a final hush, leaving him facing the city's jagged sprawl through the chill of frosted panes. The world down there can never know how close it stands to chaos, how thin the line is between disaster and the careful, clandestine unity forged here tonight. There will be no rest—only vigilance, only honor, only the brotherhood.

The marble desk occupies the heart of the penthouse study, hard and seamless—a stage polished for war. Afternoon sunlight seeps through tall glass, blurring the blue edge of the city and catching in the scattered documents Lucien now spreads with deliberate hands. The hum of sealed air whispers against Orion's pressed shirt; the rustle of court files follows Lucien as he claims his place before the glass. His shadow falls long and measured. Elara stands half a step back, fingertips leaving faint crescents on the paper edge. The leather seat behind her presses against her calves, but she won't sit.

Lucien's voice carries without force. "The prosecution's likely approach is a character arc: paint the family as unstable, the environment unpredictable. They'll press for evidence—not just fact, but impact." He lays out a photograph—Nova in her third-grade art show, paint dusting her cheeks, unsmiling. The image isn't meant to soften but to render vulnerability. "Their goal: emotional fracture. We have to counter with emotional integrity. Poignant details. Specifics. Not rehearsed answers."

Light slides across the desk's glass, fracturing in the tired glare of Orion's laptop. He leans in, jaw set, as Lucien walks through courtroom choreography—a battle plan for cynicism and sentiment. Orion's thumb hovers over a speck on the keyboard, indecision flickering before he closes the laptop with a gentle, final snap.

Elara grips the chill of the window frame, watching the city lurch under drifting clouds. The city outside feels far away, untouchable, as though what happens here won't ripple beyond the glass. Her breath shortens, pulse strange in her throat. She wants to step away, but Lucien's gaze is level, waiting.

"Let's walk through possible cross-examination." Lucien doesn't smile. It would seem like permission to lie. "Elara, how would you answer if they ask why Nova hasn't returned to school since the last incident?"

Her mouth dries, tongue slow. "I—Nova's anxiety…" She fumbles with the word, voice too thin. "She's been… frightened by the changes. It isn't about hiding her; it's about giving her room to recover. With support, she—"

Orion's fist clenches, knuckles whitening, but he stays silent.

"She needs structure. Safety. Not scrutiny," Elara finishes, her voice breaking a little. Her knees threaten to buckle. She forces herself to anchor, fingers seeking a slip of notes from the table. The paper is warmed by her skin, stiff with penciled reminders: Nova is not evidence.

"Again," Lucien says, measured. "Let your answer rest on what Nova needs. Not what the public expects. Don't cede that ground."

A silence, softer than before. Elara reads her own looping handwriting, feeling her pulse begin to slow. Across the desk, Orion watches—a man half-chained by habit, half-buoyed by fear. His presence hums, electric and strange, pain wrapped in order. She wonders if she'll ever belong in a world run by men who schedule every crisis, who wear their battle scars discreetly behind steel and glass.

He pushes the laptop open again, and the sudden blue glow splinters across their faces. The news headlines are unkind—an image of Nova, blurred for privacy, side by side with courtroom scrawl. Orion's jaw tenses. His voice, when he calls his PR chief, rings crisp:

"Flood the socials with the family gallery—no, not staged. I want photos from yesterday, Nova's artwork everywhere. And update the statement: Focus on her resilience. She comes first."

He doesn't look at Elara, but the words glance off her anyway. A strange shield. He is reckless, but in this moment, there's a sharpness in him that dares the world to blink first.

Lucien brings the meeting to an orderly, if heavy, pause. He stacks his folders, the edges of the files sighing against each other. Papers slip, a stiff symphony in the hush. Orion relaxes his shoulders, the laptop shutting with a soft finality; Elara's notes gather in her lap, her thumb stroking the corner. Sunlight leaks around them—a fading gold across the edge of the desk, painting all their flaws with temporary warmth.

Elara reaches across—the motion tentative but strong. Her skin brushes Orion's knuckles. "I won't let them take her," she says, her voice not much more than a promise in the hush. "We fight together."

Lucien meets her eyes—a quiet promise lighting below reserve. The gesture is slight: a nod, a subtle tightening around his mouth. For all his counsel, his real offering is the steadiness that lingers in silence.

In the space between words, there is a new type of pact forming—a frail, urgent thing. Elara senses the walls of the study recede, her doubts no longer wolfish but tamed to an ache she can bear. There is room, here, for the possibility of belonging.

Lucien leaves without ceremony, the door sealing quietly behind him as dusk claims the sky. Alone at the desk, Elara and Orion breathe into the hush, their hands still touching—tension and hope pressed close, waiting on the cusp of nightfall.

Elara steps from the echoing hush of the corridor, methodically shifting the stack of bills and newsletters tucked under her arm. The penthouse foyer is still, its marble veins traced with fading daylight. As she reaches for the keypad to rearm the security alarm, her gaze snags on a pale envelope perched in shadow beneath the door. No wax seal, just rough block letters scraping across its surface—her name, ragged and urgent. She kneels, fingers trembling a little despite herself, recalling the weight of a note slipped into Nova's backpack days before. Anonymous threats have become phantoms trailing her every step—warnings cloaked in childish handwriting, encrypted orders hissing from untraceable screens. She's learned to expect the chill that settles under her skin, but it never stops feeling personal.

She tears the flap open. Inside, a single sheet. Ink as black as obsidian slices through the page with the precision of a scalpel: THE BROTHERHOOD'S GLASS TOWERS WILL CRACK. PROTECT THE CHILD IF YOU CAN. The words ripple, their menace vibrating in the silence—a summoning of every nightmare that's haunted her sleep since Nova's first panic attack and the cryptic whisper, Watch the shadows in your own house. Every muscle in her body braces as if against a coming storm.

Orion stands in the kitchen beyond the foyer, the blue glow of his phone cast up into hard lines beneath his eyes, his thumb scrolling through a never-ending stream of legal briefings and media outrage. Elara enters, the note level in her hand. Quiet shakes mask the tremor in her voice. "Orion. Someone left this."

He reads in silence. His jaw tightens, eyes narrowing to slits—an animal cornered, prideful and afraid. He doesn't hesitate, doesn't ask if it's just a prank. Orion immediately dials Darius. The Brotherhood's fortress, for all its polished stone and panoramic windows, is only as strong as its keepers. Darius's voice comes through, slow and steady, background noise of surveillance screens and humming equipment. Orion's tone sharpens, becoming all clipped orders and threat: "Lock down every entrance. Pull feeds, sweep the exterior. Station extra guards. I want whoever left that found in the next hour."

He ends that call, thumbs through his directory for Caius. On speaker, the city's night noises tumbling in from a distant car as Caius answers—no surprise, only a calculated, dark humor stitched between pauses. "Send a copy. I'll scrub the mailroom feeds. No one slips in or out unseen. We tighten everything. You're not alone. Not now."

Elara's heart pounds out a fast, sick rhythm, urgent and hollow. Old fears crowd in—the fear she'll mess up, that her best won't be enough the next time Nova's innocence is endangered. She forces them down, tries to steady her breathing. The kitchen smells faintly of burnt coffee and citrus cleaner, antiseptic aromas failing to banish the sense of threat curling in the air.

A soft rustle. Nova appears at the edge of the hall, feet in fluffy socks almost too quiet for the marble, eyes wide and shining beneath a fringe of tangled hair. There is nothing theatrical in the child's fear—just that deep tremble Elara knows too well, the silent retreat of a skittish animal sensing danger long before words are spoken. Nova seizes Elara's hand, clutching so tight Elara feels each heartbeat through the small palm. The note is instantly forgotten. Instinct overpowers strategy—Elara drops to her knees, smoothing trembling strands of hair behind Nova's ear.

"It's going to be all right, sweetheart," she whispers, her voice soft like the hush of the sea at dusk, "You're safe, you hear? Nothing's getting through these walls. Not while we're here." Nova doesn't answer, but after a moment, her rigid body vents a shudder, and her breath evens, the panic edged back—not banished, but held at bay.

Upstairs, the Brotherhood responds in kind—Caius sets up a video call, Lucien's face stony, Darius's eyes flickering with a rare worry, two more supporters grim and silent. Their surroundings blur into the background: brick, glass, clandestine tech blinking like tiny stars in a constellation of control. Together, they dissect the message, voices low and calm, each syllable tightening the invisible net they've spread over their allies. It's not only Orion or Nova. The Brotherhood's shadow is long; the threat, molecular, bleeding into every corner of their world. They are no longer bastions of secrecy—their glass towers, once symbols of strength, now potential targets marked for ruin.

Downstairs, the penthouse grows dim as Orion closes the envelope in a steel lockbox, hands steady but pale. The only light comes from a security panel pulsing quietly in the gloom—a reminder that protection is never complete, only fortified anew at every fresh warning.

A hush settles in the master bedroom, the city's after-midnight rain leaving ghosts of light shimmering across the marble sill. The futuristic skyline stretches beyond the glass walls—cold, indifferent. Inside, warmth glows only from a single bedside lamp, throwing pale ambers across Orion's tense frame. He sits, still dressed, on the edge of the bed: shirt wrinkled, hands clamped so tightly his knuckles blanch, watching the floor as if searching for answers hidden in the grain. Shadows pool around his feet.

Elara pauses at the doorway, her bare feet sinking noiselessly into the thick blue rug. For a heartbeat, neither speaks. The only sound is the city's distant hush, wind chafing glass ten stories below, then a faint metallic echo as Orion's watchband creaks under his restless thumb. He lifts his gaze—no armor in his eyes now, only something raw and stripped down, bracing for the blow.

"Elara," he murmurs, voice pulled thin. "What if we're not enough? What if they win—take Nova—what's left of any of this?" His laugh is dry, almost bitter. "Every time I start to believe this could be... something real. Something I won't lose. The world finds another way to break it."

She crosses to him, slow, careful as if skirting electrical wire. The lamplight paints soft arcs across her cheekbones, dark eyes keen. She kneels beside him, close enough that the heat between their bodies gathers and grows. Orion stares at his clasped hands. His shoulders tense—memories pressing down: his sister's funeral, the judge's gavel, headlines screaming his failures in digital ink. Each moment adds another stone to his chest.

He dreams sometimes—vivid, vicious things. The city flooding, Brotherhood towers crumbling, Nova's hand wrenched from his—her voice calling uncle, fading as lawyers, cameras, the world devour whatever hope he'd built from chaos and grief.

"I keep thinking," Orion mutters, words splintering, "maybe there's a version where I don't screw this up. A future that's not just damage control. But I don't know how to hold on to it." The lamplight catches the silver at his temples, the old scar along his forearm, every sign of fight and flight.

Elara sits on the bed beside him, fingers curling over his. Her touch is cool, gentle, but her grip is fierce.

"You won't lose her," she says. "Not if I can help it. But I'm scared too, Orion." Her voice wavers just a little, the admission costing her. She looks at the wall—the swirl of city lights beyond it—then back at him, steady. "Sometimes I'm terrified that nothing I do will be enough. That this—us, Nova, quiet days together—it'll just... vanish the next time the storm comes."

Dialogue block:

"You don't have to fix all of this yourself, you know," she whispers. "I'm not here because I was hired to stay through the easy parts. I'm not leaving, even when it's hell. But I need you to meet me there. In the honesty. In the mess."

He stares at her, unblinking. "I don't know if I can promise to be the man you deserve. The world doesn't want people like us to win, Elara. We're chaos. I'm chaos."

Her smile is small but unyielding. "Then let's build something with it. Stability isn't the absence of storms. It's learning how to weather them together. That's my promise. As long as you want this—want us—I'm not going anywhere."

Orion draws a breath, shaky but new, and lets go of his hands—lets them rest, at last, open and still. Silence rises between them, not empty but electric, humming with all the words they can't quite give shape to. Elara leans in, her head resting on his shoulder. His arm slides around her without thinking, fingers threading through her hair. The city is muffled, all sharpness dulled by the thick walls and their joined presence.

It occurs to Orion, for the very first time, that hope might not be a liability. That letting her see his fractured edges doesn't guarantee loss. The idea is alien—almost laughable. But possible. He imagines—speculates, despite himself—what peace could look like. A morning without dread humming beneath his skin, Nova's laughter echoing down the hallway while Elara's quiet voice reads in a sunlit corner. No lawyers, no sirens, no wolves at the door. Just breathing room.

But reality is a blade at his neck: the threat folded in the lockbox, enemies clawing at their glass fortress, the knowledge that found family is as fragile as any code he's ever tried to decrypt. Orion aches with wanting—wanting to believe Elara, to belong here.

He checks his watch—minutes slipping toward dawn, the trial's shadow stretched across tomorrow. Reluctantly, he stands, padding down the silent hall. Each step multiplies the weight and, in another way, releases it. He peeks into Nova's room: Elara smoothing the covers, Nova's breath soft with dreams, her small hand curled around a stuffed rabbit.

Orion closes the door quietly, fingers grazing the switch. The penthouse dims, only the city's luminous sprawl persisting. When he returns, Elara stands at the bedroom threshold, haloed by pale light, her silhouette quietly resolute. They exchange no words—none needed. Side by side, they face the dark, holding this peace for one more heartbeat before the storm that waits beyond the glass.

Courtroom Showdown
Part One

Lucien Blackwell's fingers, unflinching, align the stack of documents on the defense table, crisp white paper against smooth mahogany. Light glances off his tailored jacket; the room, with its high ceilings and solemn oak trim, swallows him for a breath—then gives him back, composed and precise. Silver-gray sunlight pours through the gleaming windows and paints pale rectangles across the marble floor; the city's towers burn behind glass, streaming morning into the modern courthouse. The faint scent of polish and aged paper hovers beneath the cold ventilation, a hush—a waiting, collective inhale.

The doors open with a prolonged groan. Every lawyer and board member straightens. The judge enters in charcoal robes that whisper against the stone as she climbs the steps to her bench, intent, eyes steady. The hum of whispered speculation falters. Lucien rises; Orion's gaze flickers to the shield of briefs Lucien now holds, as if those papers, dense with history and hope, might carry a fortress between this family and ruin. Beyond Lucien, the board's counsel shuffles a deck of yellow folders, grim as a dealer about to lay down the final cards.

Family courts—especially now, with whole cities watching—are not sanctuaries. Wealth and pain stack against each other; power, grief, and reputation turn private tragedies into spectacle. Within these walls, every murmur is fodder for a million screens. Every argument has an echo outside, in a world starved for a new scandal to chew.

He addresses the court with a calm inflected by bedrock resolve. Every phrase is chosen for ballast: "On February ninth of last year, Nova Vega's mother passed suddenly." The words fall, beads in a chain, weighty and full of hidden reverberation. "Mr. Orion Vega—present in the immediate aftermath, guardian by written consent and by action—filed for custodianship within three days." He speaks of the documents, the signatures secured with shaking hands in dawn's uncertain light, of a child's trembling voice asking for her uncle through feverish tears.

Board counsel shoots a glance, mouth pinched. Lucien reads the move—this volley, that counter—before it happens, meeting the stare with the impassivity of a chess master, every calculation kept close. The larger game always pulses beneath these hearings: The board doesn't want Nova mistreated; they want Orion controllable, the company image scoured of scandal. They wield rumors like clubs, fully aware that even lies take root if nourished in public soil.

He pivots, voice low and sharp. "Let us distinguish evidence from speculation. Much is made of Mr. Vega's alleged indiscretions—half-truths and edited footage distract from the task we face this morning." He returns, unfaltering, to his metrics: report cards, testimonials from Nova's teachers, physician's charts tracking her growth, the improvements mapped out in ink. The brush of Lucien's thumb over each page, the tiny click as another document slides into place, becomes a rhythm the courtroom follows.

On the judge's desk, her pen stirs, restless, noting every distinction Lucien draws. She interrupts, her voice like gravel washed in rainwater: "Counselor, clarify the child's panic episodes."

Lucien nods, not glancing at his notes. "Her panic attacks, documented since before guardianship, have decreased in both frequency and severity. She receives ongoing therapy; Mr. Vega's home supports her comfort and routine, as confirmed by her psychologist and tutor."

The judge nods once, her face unreadable. The smell in the courtroom shifts—perspiration and too-strong cologne, a latent tang of nervousness quickening from the packed pews behind the black rail. Rows of faces—some tight-lipped with sympathy, others blank, others intent as wolves—watch the line between ruin and reprieve. Beyond the rear partition's glass wall, the clatter of keyboard keys flares and dies, quick as the hush that followed the video leak weeks ago. A sketch artist glides charcoal deftly along paper, catching the angle of Lucien's jaw, the stoic curve of Orion's hands braced on the table, the smallness of Nova in her navy dress, feet swinging, anxious but quiet.

"In summary," Lucien finishes, standing at the line between shadow and sunlight, "we ask the court to see not rumor, but the reality reflected by evidence and by this child's progress. Past errors do not—should not—define the future Mrs. Vega deserves. View only the stability, safety, and the steps taken to heal, not the noise blared beyond these walls."

With that, he returns to his chair. For a moment, the judge's expression softens—almost—and she nods for the next voice to come forward, one hand already scribed with fresh notes, the tension in the room shifting, taut as a bowstring.

"Mr. Blackwell, the board has submitted phone logs—care to address those?" The question is a challenge, thinly veiled beneath impartiality.

"Of course, Your Honor," Lucien replies. "Those logs, when placed in context, simply reflect after-hours communications relating to Nova's welfare. We can provide timestamps and witness corroborations. There are no illicit dealings—just due diligence from a household thrown into crisis."

Counsel for the board leans in, lips drawn tight. "You claim stability, but what about the media—'Vega Unfit' trending for days, sponsors withdrawing—"

"Public opinion is not legal proof," Lucien counters, his voice low and flint-edged. "We deal in the welfare of a child, not flash-in-the-pan hysteria."

A camera's shutter snaps in the gallery, loud as thunder. Eyes flicker off Lucien, off Orion, back to the judge. The judge lifts her hand.

"Thank you, Counselor. Let's have the next witness."

Light flares gold and sharp through the arched windows, slanting across rows of polished pews and the slender wooden witness stand front and center. Elara Kent steps forward, her palm pressed fleetingly against her skirt to still the tremor, and takes the solemn oath. The judge, robed in stern charcoal, fixes her with a look both grave and searching. Elara feels the world narrow to the courtroom's vaulted hush—the hush of city traffic muted beyond stone, the click of a laptop in the press box, Nova's fragile silhouette sitting beside Orion, hands knotted so tightly that the knuckles blanch.

Her own fingers, curled beneath the edge of the stand, press against old nerves, memories streaking up like electricity. She's split between this moment—sun warming half her face, hundreds of eyes somewhere behind the glare—and the ghosts of her first days here: the cavernous hallways of the Vega penthouse, Nova's spectral presence, the silence in the rooms that money could not fill.

She centers herself in rhythm and detail. "The first time I met Nova," Elara begins, her voice steadier than her fluttering pulse, "she barely spoke at all. She would wake in the night calling for her mother—sometimes she didn't sleep at all. She hid, sometimes for hours, in corners or closets, afraid that anyone new would try to take her away." The air tastes faintly of dust and citrus floor wax, the bench's wood slick under her palm. She meets the judge's eyes, then glances at Nova, who watches with silent, desperate hope.

Elara's words conjure those brittle weeks—shadows under Nova's eyes, drawn curtains, the desperate cadence of a child's breathing as a panic attack crested. Step by step, she paints the path they made together: "We began with small things. The same story before bed every night, tea instead of cocoa when she was anxious, three deep breaths before breakfast. She left drawings on my desk—just scribbles at first, but one day she wrote my name beside stick figures. It started there. Trust, I've learned, isn't stormed—it's built. Slowly."

She sees herself as if from the outside. Her spine held ramrod-straight, the silk blouse prickling against suddenly damp skin. A storm brews inside her—worry and devotion and the prickle of judgment she feels from every quarter, city and boardroom and newspaper column. Elara thinks: Will these words be twisted? Will she have to watch Nova's heart break again, the way she once watched her little brother's casket lowered into red clay, her mother's hands gripping her too tightly, desperate to hold what couldn't be kept?

Her voice is soft but deliberate. "I witnessed Nova have panic attacks in her study—she'd curl up, hands shaking, unable to breathe. Together, we learned how to slow down the fear. Orion was often up at night with her, reading until she fell asleep. He cooks breakfast most mornings, if Nova asks. The routines became anchors. I watched her draw one day—a family, she wrote, and she gave the picture to me."

She pauses, letting the judge hear the catch in her breath, letting the memory hover. Light glances off courtroom marble; whispers ripple from the gallery, a tissue pressed to a listener's lips, pencils scratching hurried notes.

She draws courage from raw honesty. "I know Orion's reputation. The media—everyone—believes chaos is all he can offer. That viral video, the rumors, they haunt these proceedings. But I've never seen anyone fight harder to keep Nova safe, to give her a home. One night, Nova's panic wouldn't break—Orion sat with her until sunrise, holding her through every wave. Everything he does, despite his mistakes, is for her. Stability doesn't always look predictable from the outside—but Nova is thriving. She laughs now. She wants to learn."

In her peripheral vision, Orion sits utterly still; Nova's tiny shoulder rises and falls in time with Elara's voice.

"If you'll allow me," she says quietly, "I am not speaking as an employee this morning. I am here as someone who loves Nova and who believes with everything I have that her happiness, her healing, come from the family she has—Orion, myself, all of us together. We are her anchors." She forces herself to meet the judge's eyes a final time. "All I want is for Nova to remain where she is safest. With family."

A hush descends, unbroken except for the clack of a reporter's pen rolling to the floor and the gentle, ragged exhale Elara releases as she returns to her chair, the world restored to size but changed—her soul bare before the court, for Nova, for herself.

Nova's legs dangle, barely brushing the floor, as the bailiff kneels beside her. She holds her plush blue turtle tight, so tight her knuckles pale, fabric worn smooth under anxious little fingers. Morning sunlight slants through the arched windows, settling in pools across the flagstone floor, warming the sharp smell of polished wood and old paper. Every adult eye is a slow tide of strangers—lawyers, board members, men and women with hardly a name in her world—but there is Elara. There is Orion. Nova glances back over her shoulder, and Elara gives a slow, steady nod. Orion's hand, thumb tucked under his cuff, flickers a silent promise.

Heart pounding, shoes whispering quieter than the clocks, Nova climbs the step up to the witness box. Her mouth tastes of the vanilla from her breakfast cocoa—Orion made it himself, even though he always burned the milk. She sits small behind the vast wood, turtle pressed close like a secret talisman. The judge, austere beneath the dark sweep of her robes, leans in. The hush of keyboards rises from the gallery behind frosted glass, carrying rumors to corners Nova will never see.

The judge's voice, low but gentle, billows in the air. "Nova, do you know why you're here today?"

Nova looks down at her turtle, mouth trembling. She wants to say no, but Elara once explained that the truth was braver even when it trembled. "Because you want to know if I'm happy. If...I'm safe," she whispers.

The next question is a careful thread: How does Elara help when the bad feelings come? Nova's feet draw back under her chair; she rocks softly, thumb tracing shells on the blue plush. The courtroom vanishes for a second—replaced by the memory of Elara's hand on her back in that bright school alcove. Breathe in. Out. In. Out. When the monsters in her chest gnaw at her heart, Elara sits close and makes the world tick slow and gentle again.

"She...she helps me find my breath. She says it's like counting clouds." The words tumble out broken, but Nova clings to them the way she does Elara's consistency. "Sometimes, I get lost and it hurts here." She presses a fist to her sternum. "But she sits with me until it feels not so scary. Sometimes we draw, or...listen to music. She stays until I don't shake so bad anymore."

"And Orion?" the judge asks.

A pinch of a smile threatens. Nova's gaze swings toward her uncle. He's never still—always working or pacing or cursing at some machine under his breath—but in the deepest, hardest nights, he brings cocoa, extra marshmallows, and remembers to shut off all the bright blue lights that could upset her. "He makes cocoa when I can't sleep. He...he tells stories. Sometimes I hear him outside my room, just waiting." Her cheeks grow hot for saying so much, but in the court's charged stillness, the words seem to matter.

A hush expands. Sunlight glints off courtroom glass, finding the single thread of uncertainty wound tight in Nova's chest. She feels every gaze, but only Elara and Orion's matter. She wishes it were just them. Her fingers toy with the turtle's faded flipper, pulse racing.

Dialogue block:

"Nova, do you like where you live?" the judge asks, her voice softening.

She nods once, her voice thinner than a page. "I like it. I like being with them." Her shoes scuff together, words tumbling. "I like when Elara helps me. I like Orion reading stories. I like our breakfasts...when they're there, the house feels warm. Safer."

A board lawyer, lean and angular, clears his throat. "Nova, if you had to go somewhere else, would you be okay with that? Maybe a place with more children, or—"

Her lip quivers. "No. I'd be scared." She shakes her head, turtle crushed against her chest. "I don't want to go. I don't want to...I don't want to lose my family."

Her gaze sinks. The vastness of the room, the weight of adult silence, presses close. Voices in her head echo all the old fears: that families can fall apart, that the people who stay might not stay forever. Her language is unsure, hope balancing on a blade. The "bad feelings" swirl like storm clouds, but memory roots her—Elara humming low on anxious afternoons, Orion's fumbled pancakes, the way sunlight felt different when she believed she belonged.

She lifts her head. "If I go away...I won't have my family anymore. I'd lose my uncle. And Elara. I don't want that."

In the first row, a juror clamps a hand over their mouth, tears bright as crystal beads. Someone near the rail—maybe the therapist—quietly removes fogged glasses and wipes them, the gesture tender, protective, as if shielding Nova from the sharpness of everything grown-up. The old rhythm of questions and proof, arguments and accusations, dissolves in the gravity of a child's longing. It hangs between pillars, painting the marble with raw, vulnerable truth.

The judge does not smile but nods, her voice gentled by something only real pain can grant. "Thank you, Nova. That was very brave." She gestures to the bailiff, who bows low and holds out a hand, palm up, inviting instead of pulling.

Nova slides from the seat and hesitates. She spies Elara immediately—steady as a lighthouse, arms wide—and in a breathless burst, she runs to her, buries her face in Elara's skirt, plush turtle between them. Elara enfolds her close. Orion's hand lands gently on Nova's shoulder, warm and solid—a shield at her back. Here, in the hush after testimony, the knot binding the three of them tightens—wordless, fierce, unbreakable—while all the cold machinery of law and spectacle pauses, just for a quiet, aching heartbeat.

Outside the courthouse, the world rearranges itself into lenses and microphones. Clouds hang low, smearing the noon light into a cold silver that glances off marble and glass. Reporters huddle in crisp winter coats, badges swinging from lapels like amulets against the wind, screens blinking with fevered updates. At the top of the steps stands the newscaster whose words thread through a web of distant satellites—her voice amplified, carefully measured, plotting the morning's testimony into neat parcels fit for syndication. Threads of speculation unravel through the air. Every gesture, every pause, is spun for the hungry eyes behind the barriers.

Beyond the cordon, Evan, sharp-eyed among the horde, raises his camera. He's dressed for anonymity—gray scarf, heavy boots—one rung above the sidewalk's chaos, tracking the doors where stories emerge raw and blinking. He studies body language, waits for uncertainty. The courthouse doors groan open. Lucien strides first, measured and silent, Orion at his flank in an ink-dark suit, expression unreadable beneath practiced composure. Assistants swarm, but Evan's timing is perfect—his finger clicks the shutter as a hand thrusts a broadsheet toward Orion's face, blocking the worst of the flash. Still, a slice of Orion's wary eyes and Elara's solemn profile are immortalized, a tableau desperate for an ugly headline.

The outside noise is a living thing. Laughter and clipped instructions snap through the assembled crews as cable vans hum, diesel exhaust thickening the air. Inside their wagons, social strategists tap at keyboards, the blue light of screens painting their faces sickly. Tweets blossom with the court's hashtags—#NovaVegaCustody, #Scandal-Guardian—rising quick and wild. Someone posts a grainy photo: Orion holding Nova's small hand by the witness box, her blue turtle peeking out. Underneath, a swirl of commentary casts judgment and blessing like fickle weather. Rumors coil through the feeds: Did Elara Kent hesitate before she answered? Was Orion's silence guilt, or something deeper? The city's gossip engines grind, hot and tireless, fed by fragments and fear.

Caius emerges—a black coat, shoulders set like a fortress. The crowd parts just enough for him to appear beside Lila and Mariel, both poised on the razor's edge of visibility. Chaos vibrates beneath the polish of their presence. Lila's breath fogs in the winter air, fingertips pressing Nova's shoulder with gentle assurance.

"Do you have it?" Caius asks, his voice pitched low.

Mariel tilts her phone so Elara, flanked by Brotherhood muscle and Lila's soft calm, can see the words marching across the trending tab. She arches a brow. "Apparently, you 'confessed your secret affair with the guardian on the stand,'" she murmurs, dry as dust. "The world's already voted."

Elara's jaw tenses; the muscles flutter beneath her skin as she absorbs the venom on the screen. Lila leans closer, murmuring soft encouragement, radiating stability as if she could knit a shield around all of them with the warmth of her palm. Nova huddles against Elara, eyes huge in the sea of legs and clattering camera equipment, turtle clutched like a talisman against exile.

The Brotherhood closes ranks—silent, unyielding—forming their world's true perimeter. In the air hangs sweat, old stone, perfume, the ozone tang of oncoming rain. For a breathless moment, Orion stands isolated in the storm's eye, his shape outlined by the push of strangers and the gravity of the girl pressed to his side. Elara's hand is small but firm on Nova's shoulder, a human promise.

"Ignore it," Caius breathes, his gaze scanning for weakness in the press line. "It's noise. We hold the truth."

"Noise can become an avalanche if you're not careful," Lucien mutters, glancing over.

Orion's exterior is ice, but his pulse drums wild. He imagines each fleeting glance—the hesitation as Elara brushes Nova's hair back, the involuntary clench of his jaw—detonating across the feeds. One photo, truth twisted, and everything could disintegrate. He wonders what a board member might leak in a single email. He wonders how much faith will fracture before midnight. The Brotherhood is a wall, but he feels the cracks spidering, invisible but growing.

He pictures headlines that warp love into scandal, that drag his failures out and crucify Elara with them. He is tired of dodging ghosts. Still, he wants to believe that protecting them—Nova, Elara, this patchwork tribe—means more than optics or victory in court. Some battles are elemental and raw, fought in the hush behind closed doors and in the storm that follows outside. Responsibility presses in, almost physical, heavy as the city's tallest tower. His mistakes glow on every screen, weaponized by strangers. All those restless nights mourning his sister, holding Nova close and promising safety, seem so small now—yet they're the only thing real.

Lucien's phone vibrates—a digital rattle that cuts through it all. He reads the message, lips pressed white. Without a word, Lucien turns the screen for Orion: Empires collapse under the harsh light. Are you ready to defend yours?

Orion meets Lucien's gaze, the air suddenly colder. The swelling mob, the unfurling rumors, the relentless light—none of it abates as the Brotherhood leads their fragile family into the safety of the courthouse foyer, cameras strobing in their wake.

Courtroom Showdown
Part Two

The courtroom feels both cavernous and claustrophobic—the sort of space where words echo longer than their weight, and the polished wood glows under autumn's late light, filtering through arched panes. Lucien Blackwell's footsteps drum softly on gray stone as he approaches the podium, case files balanced precisely in his hands, glasses catching the glimmer from a thousand watchful eyes. Around him, rows of benches hum with anticipation, a nervous expectancy sharp as ozone before a storm.

He looks first to the judge, then to the gallery—a crowd comprised of local press, boardroom stalwarts, and a few ordinary souls, drawn like moths to the glow of city drama. Somewhere in the middle, Elara sits, knuckles whitening over folded hands, her composure a shield that could shatter at the wrong syllable. Nova's small figure leans into Orion, whose dark silhouette stands out like a warning or a vow.

Lucien's voice, when it comes, is measured velvet with an under-current of iron.

"Your Honor," he begins, sliding a thumb over the top of the file, as if to remind himself of everything that rests beneath it, "we are not here because of a business transaction or a board directive. We are here because a child's life—her sense of safety, her fragile hope—hangs in the balance." He glances at Nova, who meets his gaze with eyes too old for any eight-year-old to carry.

He details the proof: records of Nova's therapy, tuition banked and scheduled without fail, receipts for home security upgrades, psychiatrist letters, and meticulously chronicled evidence of stability. "Mr. Vega's actions speak through more than figures," Lucien continues. "They manifest in bedtime rituals, in quiet cups of cocoa shared on stormy nights, in every careful plan to support Nova's healing. Miss Kent, who has become more than an employee—a steady rock amid the shifting storms—provides the consistency this child requires. And the child has thrived."

On the table between Orion and Nova, a navy blue folder sits un-opened. Nova's fingers graze its edge, fidgeting—her tell when anxiety prickles through. Orion covers her hand gently. A breath, subtle but perceptible, steadies her.

The city's air—the scent of ink, near-rain, and a faint trace of cologne from opposing counsel—hangs heavy in the room. Lucien sees the faces hungry for a spectacle: reporters clutching their digital devices, tongues primed for spin. Out there, perception is currency and reality negotiable. Every headline bends the truth just enough to sell another ad, another click. Here, in this airless box, it becomes legal artillery.

The board's attorney rises abruptly, voice slicing through Lucien's as though to draw blood. "Your Honor, I request the court examine

Mr. Vega's recent… regrettable conduct." A tabloid printout slides across the table—blaring headlines, grainy images, scandal pressed into every pixel, each accusation slick with manufactured outrage.

"Is this the standard for legal guardianship?" the attorney demands, raising a brow toward the press and, quietly, toward those whose checks carved this battle line.

Lucien does not flinch. He pivots, one hand resting lightly atop the defense file. "With respect, this fixation on curated scandal ignores the daily reality of Nova's existence. The inconsistencies of the board's own witnesses—and I urge Your Honor to notice the conflict between their sworn statements—undercut their credibility. What matters is the demonstrable well-being of this child. Here is the truth: Nova is safest and happiest in the care of those who have stood with her through fear, trauma, and loss. The support system built around her is deliberate—Miss Kent's commitment, Mr. Vega's unwavering presence, all verifiable, all visible in the girl herself."

His words gather gravity, drawn from a well deeper than statutory law. He feels the pressure—a city's worth of expectation, the Brotherhood's hopes, precarious faith in the process of justice. Years of watching verdicts bend beneath the weight of old money and sharper knives leave him wary but determined.

Elara's voice is not heard, but her posture—rigid, bracing, her gaze fixed on the judge—speaks for her. Orion's arm curls protectively around Nova. The child's lashes tremble.

"For the sake of the child, Your Honor. Not the gossip. Not punitive retribution cloaked as public virtue," Lucien closes.

The judge leans back. Her gaze moves from Lucien to Orion to Elara, then Nova—a careful, leaden sweep, as if measuring what isn't itemized in the evidence.

"I am calling a recess," she states, resonant as thunder. "Both sides, submit your summations and all associated documentation. This court will reconvene soon." Her eyes linger just a fraction longer on Nova before she rises, gravity rolling in her wake.

The bailiffs move forward, ushering both legal teams toward side doors. The gallery stirs, a soft wind of murmurs and shifting feet. Reporters scrape notes, hunched by the aisle—eyes alight, hungry for fracture.

Nova clings to Orion's sleeve, her head pressed to his arm. Orion smooths her hair, whispering against the hush. Elara, one row away, doesn't move. The table—once the center of battle—is now an island afloat in uncertainty.

The city outside—in all its neon veins and whisper networks—waits for what story will be carved from the day's sweat and heartbreak. Inside, as the chamber empties, found family sits ringed by silence, understanding too well that here, victory or loss is never just personal. It echoes on every level where image haunts truth and love must fight to be recognized as real.

The door to the courtroom opens with a groan that seems too loud for the expecting hush. The judge glides to her seat as though she rides on the breath of the gathered crowd. Afternoon sunlight siphons through the tall windows, gilding her robe and the curled woodwork of the bench in reluctant gold. The air prickles—not with warmth, but with the pulse of tension, a current that raises every hair and dries every mouth.

Nova sits ramrod-straight at the defense table, her tiny fist nested in Orion's larger hand. His grip is gentle yet fiercely sure, an anchor to steady a ship in the storm. Elara's nails press half-moons into her skin; she can taste metal beneath her tongue, and each inhale is careful, measured—an act of discipline, not relief.

"All rise." The bailiff's voice is a tonic—bracing, almost electric. Everyone rises. Orion catches, for a moment, the reflection of himself and Nova in the glassy court doors; the image flickers, fractured by movement. He holds Nova's gaze, then braces his own posture, shoulders aligned and jaw locked tight.

The judge's gaze slices through the haze. Her voice is low, unwavering, as she pronounces the ruling, every syllable landing like the flutter of thunderous pages closing a chapter. Guardianship remains with Orion Vega. "This court finds the evidence overwhelming: the child's welfare—her sense of love, her path to healing—are inseparable from the nurturing she receives in this home," she says, her eyes shifting from Orion to Elara. "But let this victory rest on the condition of ongoing stability. This storm is not entirely weathered."

Relief tastes strange; mingled in the sweat and fear is something bitter, something metallic. Orion feels it gather beneath his ribs. The gallery breaks into stifled murmurs, feet shifting against aged stone. The press are wolves at the far door, pens already scraping. Lucien edges over, a signal in his eyes for privacy. He holds up a sealed pouch, the shape of which is all too familiar—a child's music box, ornate enough to trick the unwary.

"In here, please," Lucien murmurs, not waiting for debate. Orion rises, not letting go of Nova's hand until they reach the doorway. Elara touches Nova's hair, then presses after them. The corridor hums with whispers and the hot scent of anticipation—the breath of a city obsessed with power, ready to gorge itself on another family's drama.

They slip into a narrow conference room, the kind that hums with old paper, ozone from tired lamps, and the faint bite of cleaning solvent. Revolving shadows cross the frosted glass as reporters pace like sharks. Lucien closes the door, leaving the world out.

The pouch thuds onto the polished table. Lucien's words are taut, scarcely above a whisper. "Security found this in Nova's bag. It wasn't there this morning."

The music box is heavy, its filigreed edges dulled by the prints of too many anxious hands. Orion pulls on latex gloves—habit now, the cost of paranoia. He opens the box as Elara leans in, her breath trembling against its gilded rim. The familiar tune nearly begins, but Orion stops the spindle with a precise touch. He turns it over to show the marks—scratches, minute and intentional, running along the base in a scrawled crescent.

"There's a seam," Elara points, kneeling so her eye is level with the box. Her voice has the calm of someone defusing a bomb. Their shoulders nearly touch as, together, they tease open a hidden compartment, exposure revealing more than just clever clockwork. Tucked inside is a transmitter no larger than a grain of rice, black as spilled ink.

Lucien squints, his brow furrowed. "There's engraving." The words require angling the metal to the light: Every empire falls from within. The phrase is as cold and final as a grave marker, each letter scraped with absolute intention.

A chill slithers up Orion's spine. Victory, if this is what it's called, buzzes with threat. He can win a courtroom, out-argue boardrooms, buy time with money and charm—but this is different. The enemy wears no face, speaks through children's toys, haunts the quietest, most intimate corners of his life. Even Nova's innocence is no barrier. Protection is perpetual vigilance, a borderless fight. His heart hammers painfully—fear for Nova, guilt that she's again marked for harm by association with him. The scent of Elara—citrusy, steady—intersects with the metallic tang of dread.

Elara's eyes linger on Orion, reading the tension in his fisted hands, the way his breathing strains. She mirrors his resolve, her own terror crystallizing into grim determination. For once their walls are down, an unspoken bond sparking between them. She understands now that safety is more fragile than she once allowed herself to believe, that her place here—beside Nova, beside Orion—is not just a matter of duty, but survival. They stand shoulder to shoulder, not just co-guardians, but co-conspirators against the shadows pressing closer.

Outside, voices rise—reporters scenting blood or celebration; it's hard to know which. Inside, the three share a weighted silence, hunted by possibilities. Lucien paces, already strategizing in clipped, muttered fragments, while Orion and Elara linger by the music box, gravity binding them together in the space where triumph and fear are inseparable.

The city at night sprawls below, veins of neon bleeding through rain-streaked glass. Inside the Brotherhood's safe house, the lights are low, shadows pooling at the corners, giving the conference room a submarine hush. Twin towers blink promises of vigilance and threat beyond armored windows, and the faint metallic scent of ozone from overworked servers filters into the air.

Lucien, Orion, and Elara pause after stepping inside—shoulders taut, eyes still rimmed with the anxiety of the courtroom. Caius sits planted at the head of the long table, angular in navy and bone, his fingers drum-tapping a printed list beside a cascade of projected threat reports. Darius stands near the window, a broad silhouette against city lights, gaze distant but alert.

Caius slides the paper toward Orion, the list catching under a pool of LED blue. His voice is soft but edged. "Intercepted this batch since noon. Three new variants on the Helios threat—subtle tweaks. Whoever's moving against us is watching from inside."

Orion's hand fists around his cuff, knuckles pale under the wash of light. "So the board's leaks weren't the work of an outsider?"

"Not unless outsiders know our internal ciphers," Caius replies, his eyes meeting Orion's, then flicking toward Elara. "They timed the transmission with the verdict. That's coordination, not coincidence."

Darius leans forward, his voice steady. "We need to circle ranks. Whoever they are—they knew Nova's routine, when the music box would pass through security, how to blend with the press and the crowd."

Lucien crosses to the whiteboard, uncapping a marker with a click that echoes, sharp and purposeful. He draws a timeline—arrows, color-coded names, dots converging on tonight's date.

"The pattern started a month back," Lucien says, his voice low. "First, the viral leaks. Then the anonymous tips—always a day before a major event. Today, the bug in Nova's music box. Everything escalates when guardianship is at risk."

Orion stands abruptly, chair legs scraping a harsh note. "If they want to break me, they'll find I don't bend. Nova is family. I will protect her—at any cost."

Elara rises beside him, her words ringing with conviction. "She's not alone. Neither are you."

Lucien turns from the board, resolve flickering through the lines of his face. "Then we make it official. No one in this circle stands alone—we defend each other, no matter what we're up against."

A hush settles. Server fans hum, the city pulsing on the far side of thick glass. In this room, hearts quicken. Hands brush across the table—an unspoken vow moving from steel to flesh and back again.

Suddenly, every device on the table vibrates—a mechanical chorus breaking the silence. Screens ignite simultaneously, throwing a cold glow across their faces:

You survived the verdict.

The storm breaks soon.

Choose who you trust.

For a heartbeat, no one moves. The words burn in blue clarity, reflected in glassy eyes and polished steel.

*

The silent gravity in the room deepens. Lucien tracks every flicker in the others' faces—the momentary narrowing of Caius's eyes, the subtle tension sharpening Orion's jaw, Elara's hand clenching by the dark wood. He feels the old roil of responsibility in his gut, heavy and restless. Each threat, each calculated attack, peels back another sliver of Brotherhood trust. He knows the architecture of their unity: it is powerful, but not unbreakable.

What if someone's already inside, fraying the seams from within? Could it be a lover, a friend, someone looking for leverage and blinded by fear? All their careful vetting, history shared in blood and promise, and yet—so simple for one weak link to fail.

Lucien wonders about names—trusted associates whose expressions, lately, linger a beat too long. Could a plea deal or a whispered threat turn loyalty to betrayal? Would Nova become a pawn in a game none of them can see? He feels a chill along his spine; the cost of misjudging trust could sweep away everything they've built.

He weighs each ally's strengths in his mind, recalling past sacrifices—Orion's reckless perseverance, Darius's steady presence, Caius's keen scrutiny. But vulnerability trickles in. If even one gives in to fear, coerced or seduced by Helios's shadow, then every sacrifice, every defense is sand swept by storm tide.

Lucien's fingers dig into the marker. The line between defense and failure is vanishingly thin. Failure here isn't an option—not with Nova's future at stake, not with the Brotherhood's legacy backlit by the threat-blotted city.

Resolve hardens behind his chest: he will be the shield, even if the cost is his own peace. He cannot see every angle, cannot guarantee even the most fortified walls will not crack. But he'll stand in the breach, as long as he draws breath, even as doubt scrapes against bone.

The screens flicker, blue and ominous, and the oath in the air becomes a living thing—fragile but fierce. In this moment, the Brotherhood stands as one, eyes bright in the half-light, bracing for the gathering storm beyond their guarded sanctuary.

New Family and New Storms

The city never truly sleeps, but at this hour, the penthouse towers over a world of quiet. Orion, sleeves rumpled, sits beneath the glare of his study's clinical white light, his eyes stinging as digital rain cascades down his laptop screen. Within the polished glass and cold steel, all is silence except for the low hum of a ventilation vent and the restless tap of a gold-capped pen against a budget printout. Orion pores over the figures: the Vega Foundation's legendary reserves, profits stacked like dominoes, yet each dollar is about to become something else. He marks a page, swipes to another spreadsheet, murmurs under his breath, and dials his chief accountant, his voice low and urgent: "Pull the discretionary column under infrastructure. No, more. All of it—a full shift to the Kent Project, line by line." He circles the figure again, daring himself not to flinch.

Across the marble desk, ledgers fan out like wings—testaments to years of innovation, acquisition, and the heady drive to disrupt before the world could predict his next move. But now, the old hunger feels hollow when stacked against the fragile promise of a different legacy. Orion's pauses stretch—he inhales the scent of ink, ozone, and old coffee, his gaze sliding across Nova's hand-drawn portrait taped to the screen: three stick figures under a paper sun. The simple assurance of it, the innocence, catches him every time.

In the depth of night, he flicks on a secure connection. Caius's image shimmers to life on the projected wall, his hair tousled, sharp eyes catching the glint of numbers and pie charts. Orion's voice cracks with fatigue and something more vulnerable. "It's not just PR, Caius. If we anchor the rebrand on educational reform—real structure, not a headline—we're rewriting the story from the inside." He raps his knuckles on the glass, restless. "Don't let the board worry about optics. Let them see the future belongs to those who build it right."

Caius, ever the game theorist, leans back, appraising. "Stability plays better now than spectacle, Orion. You double the funding; there's public goodwill—but the stakes rise. Every audit, every rival, every shadow will dig deeper. Are you ready for that exposure?"

"I have to be." Orion's tone is unvarnished, resolve edged with the fear of being seen and found wanting. "It's Elara's vision. It's Nova's safety. It's..." He trails off. "Send the release. By noon."

Caius nods, faint respect flickering across his features. "Then we move. It's a pivot worthy of every single headline."

After the call, Orion sits back, letting the tension flood from his shoulders, the laptop illuminating old scars on his forearm. He is a builder, guardian, and shield—and for the first time in years, he is scared of the weight those words carry.

The world outside this penthouse remains hungry. Tech titans build futures atop glass towers, promises breaking as easily as crystal under a hard stare. Billionaires spark revolutions; they rarely vow permanence. But tonight, the rules distort—Orion's recalibration begins to echo in unfamiliar circles. In corridors of power and on comment boards, skepticism and hope swirl: who is a disruptor, if not a repairman? What does it mean for the old guard if even Vega turns from chaos to stewardship? The status quo shifts; so do the shadows that thrive in upheaval. Every redirected million is an invitation to scrutiny or sabotage—but also a blueprint for others fumbling toward legacy over legend. Now, the myth of Orion Vega veers—a story rewritten not on the promise of tomorrow's technology, but on the lasting shelter of steadfastness.

Exhaustion gnaws, but Orion cannot retreat from this edge. The risk, the rawness—he channels it into meticulous organization, printing the thick packet of documents: projected costs, phased implementation charts, a letter of intent bearing both his signature and a space left for the woman who has, against reason, become his anchor. He slides everything into a folder embossed with the Vega crest and places it on the coffee table beneath the soft white pendant lamp, precise as an offering.

He fires off a message—Elara, 7 a.m., study. Important.

Dawn slips in like a ghost, painting the sky and skyscraper in diluted gold. Elara arrives with her chin set and her eyes trained on the folder, her posture taut yet open. In the hush, she breaks the seal, pages whispering as she flips from number to letter to vision—her pulse beating high in her throat. Orion waits, hands braced on the armchair, watching her eyes widen as she grasps the depth of his commitment.

"The scope..." she breathes out, almost soundless. "This is—Orion, this is more than I even asked for."

"My team will support you. You can take the lead—if you want it." His voice, rough with nerves, cracks the calm between them. He catches her gaze, letting her see everything he is—imperfect, reckless, trying.

Elara studies him, resolve and gratitude entwined. "I want partnership," she replies simply. "Not handouts. And I need to know boundaries—yours and mine—will be respected. We build this only if we do it as equals. For Nova, for everyone."

He nods, relief and fear knotted tight. "Yes. Together."

Outside the window, morning splits the city into promise and peril. Elara sets her hand atop the proposal—no trembling, only the firm certainty of choice. Her smile, small but real, cuts through the remains of old distance, anchoring them both as the world tilts toward something starkly, stubbornly new.

Evening spills gold across the penthouse, painting the sharp lines of glass and steel in forgiving light. Outside, the city flickers with life below, barely muffled by the hush inside Vega's fortress. The living room, usually cavernous and cool, now feels smaller. Softer. Elara settles onto the navy sofa, her knees drawn together, fingers knotted in her lap. She has the unspoken look of someone bracing for impact but determined all the same—the steadiness of a mountain enduring the wind.

Orion drifts in from the hallway, the faintest scents of cinnamon and toast clinging to him, vestiges of breakfast with Nova. His stride is easier than in days past, his shoulders no longer hunched by storm. With a controlled exhale, he lowers himself onto the other end of the sofa, close but not encroaching. For a moment, they sit in companionable silence, only the rhythmic hum of distant traffic and the occasional sharp bark from the German Shepherd at the far end of the penthouse breaking the quiet.

Elara studies the way the morning sun frames Orion, his profile carved in silver and shadow. Here, in this sanctuary of money and modernity, the rules keep shifting under her feet. He's a man built for chaos, his life a clockwork of risk and reinvention, while she's fashioned herself out of order, certainty, and unyielding lines. Still, she has seen the way his hands shake when Nova's voice trembles, the way he guards vulnerability like a cracked diamond. Their volatility, she thinks, is both their storm and—maybe, if she dares—a kind of hope.

She straightens, her voice measured. "Before we go further, we need to talk about how this works. If I'm going to stay, it can't be as an employee. I don't want to exist on the margins of your life, stepping around your grief or your impulses." The words are crisp, but her gaze carries weight, layered with both fear and longing. "This only works if we're honest. You don't get to shut me out when things turn ugly. And Nova needs routine. Stability. Not just bursts of attention between crises."

Orion's jaw tightens, and his fingers toy with his cufflinks—habitual, restless. He looks away, out toward the shimmering city. "You think I haven't wanted that? Half the time, I'm fighting to keep the ground from caving in. I know I make things messy. I'll admit that." His laughter is brittle, a glittering edge undercut by regret. "Consistency isn't my strong suit. But if it's what Nova needs... and what you need... I'm willing to try. Not just say it. Do it."

Elara holds his gaze, testing for fault lines that might give way. She recognizes the anxiety in his posture—the way his shoulders stiffen before confession, the stubborn pride locked behind his eyes. "I need an equal say. About Nova. About the house. About... us. If you want family, not just someone to patch the leaks when things get rough, then you have to meet me at the table. If you can't, tell me now."

Dialogue settles between them, as fragile as spun glass.

"I can't promise I'll never screw up," Orion says, his voice sliding low. "I don't know if I'll ever stop running sometimes. But I'm done shutting you out. I don't want to lose either of you. Especially not because I was an idiot who couldn't ask for help."

"Running's not the problem, Orion. Hiding is." Elara lets herself bend, just a little. "If you say you'll stay, you have to mean it. For her, and maybe for you, too."

He laughs, softer this time. "You drive a hard bargain, Kent."

"You're impossible," she murmurs, but the slightest upturn of her lips betrays her.

The hush returns heavy and sweet, a peace wrought from necessity and battle both. Their hands drift closer, almost touching—fingertips ghosting over polished leather, not quite brave enough for more. Elara feels the echo of her own pulse, the old ache of risk, of the cost of caring, pressing at her ribcage. She knows what loss tastes like—dry copper, echoing hollow into the years. Still, she reaches for his hand, letting the warmth settle between their palms for the briefest, precious span.

This is what she has learned: boundaries can be porous, and trust is grown in inches, not leaps. Her discipline is not armor but an invitation—a way to hold safe the things that matter. Yet, letting him in, even a step, raises specters of all she could lose again. She can hear the ghost-echoes of past betrayals in her blood, warning her against hope, but Nova's laughter from down the hall buoys her beyond fatalism. Here, in the golden spill of this moment, she tastes the beginning of something fragile and hard-won—a new shape for love, uneasy but real.

She releases him, just enough to regain control. "I'll stay." Her voice is steady as stone and soft as velvet, the terms clear. "But I stay as family. Trust me with the truth, even when it's ugly. I need that. Nova needs that."

He squeezes her hand before she can pull away. "We'll do this together. One day at a time."

Light expands in the room, the city outside blooming, and the old rules quietly dissolve.

Sunlight spills through the narrow windows of the Brotherhood headquarters, glinting off Caius's mahogany desk, landing on orderly files and half-drained espresso. His phone vibrates once, insistent and cold against his palm—across town, Lucien's phone lights up in his book-lined home office, its precise chime slicing through the soft classical notes from his speakers. Darius, fresh from a call in his kitchen where the scent of roasted coffee and lemon bread lingers, catches the message mid-swipe, his eyes tightening with each word. Orion, curled in his penthouse library nook surrounded by the silent histories of technology and myth, stiffens as the same encrypted alert appears on his screen. The message is terse, unadorned: THE ARCHIVE OPENS IN 60 DAYS. CHOOSE WHAT TO PROTECT.

In four corners of the city, four men absorb the warning in brittle stillness. Caius, ever the tactician, narrows his eyes, his thumb tapping the screen as if the algorithm might yield to pressure. Lucien's gaze traces the signature embedded in the code, seeking familiar handprints, the scentless echo of old adversaries—a puzzle, half-known, lurking beneath the surface. Darius lets out a breath so slow it blurs the air, his broad fingers curling into his palm as he leans back. In the penthouse, Orion's jaw clenches, his knuckles blanching where the light catches his wedding band—Nova's voice drifts faintly down the hall, innocence on the edge of a world that promises nothing.

Their routine video call launches with no preamble, only the drawn faces of men now linked by more than shared secrets—a network caught in a widening snare.

"This goes beyond personal. Whoever's behind this, they're not playing for leverage anymore," Caius says, his voice low, every word measured. The mahogany behind him takes on the hue of frost.

Darius nods, his usually placid eyes fierce today. "The countdown's no bluff. Someone's ready to burn everything down if we don't watch it."

Lucien's voice threads through, deep and controlled, each syllable honed by practice in courtrooms and clean, expensive offices. "Digital lockout on all files, my end. I'll double forensics on the company servers and pull client logs. Has anyone seen cross-traffic since the trial?"

Orion's eyes flicker, and it's clear he hasn't slept—not really. "A few noise pings in the secondary subsidiary. Someone poked around near the Nova trust. Nothing tripped, but it felt... familiar."

There's a hush, broken only by static and the hiss of air from Caius's side.

"This isn't a fracture," Darius breaks in. "It's a siege. Whoever Helios put in play—I think they want the Brotherhood visible, not just wounded. It's exile or exposure."

Orion leans forward until the lines of his face twist in shadow. "They want the world to watch us unravel. All of us. Not just me. Not just Nova." His voice shudders for a moment before he wrestles control back, his eyes darting to the half-open door behind him.

Caius's tone shifts, more urgent now. "We need an off-grid sit-down. Discrete. Phones dropped. Lucien, set up the protocols. Orion, can you sweep for external bugs again? Darius, reroute personal contacts and pulse security on the kids' schools. We have to expect escalation."

Darius murmurs assent, his knuckles tapping a slow rhythm on his mug. Lucien's response is prompt; Caius, always the conductor, draws the arc: "No paper. No digital trail. Nothing stays in the tower."

Orion glances down at his phone. He wants to hurl it against the hard glass, watch it shatter and bleed codes onto the marble, but instead, he just nods, finality flattening his bravado.

The call ends in a silence that reverberates through cables and open rooms.

Elsewhere, the unseen current swells. Seraphina opens a secure chat, pearls of sweat collecting along her brow as she glances at the pale sunlight reflected in her screen. Mariel, fingers flying over the keyboard from her loft, types, "Saw the message. Feels coordinated—not a random leak, but a controlled detonation. Anyone else sense it?"

Lila ghosts into the chat. "Darius is on edge. He'd never say it, but he is. Let's keep close tabs. Elara—how is Nova after the trial?"

Elara's reply lands with steady grace: "She's quieter. Watching us. If the men crumble, so does she. We need to keep order, for them. For ourselves, too."

Seraphina: "Let's set up a weekly routine—switch supervision, keep everyone grounded. Don't give Helios an opening."

Four women, four separate rooms, four steady flames against the cold. The sisterhood threads itself tighter.

The hours tick forward, and the Brotherhood's promise hangs in the air, taut as a live wire—move before the archive opens, shield what matters, let no shadow catch them off guard this time.

The women's chat signs off too, just another piece of invisible scaffolding braced against the coming storm, their families' routines quietly adjusted, eyes sharper, hands steadier, hearts refusing panic. The city hums on, unaware beneath the vaulted, watching sky.

Night deepens outside Carver Media Tower, the city below transformed into a shifting mesh of neon and rain-wet blacktop. Silas stands framed by glass that runs floor to ceiling, his silhouette sharp against the cold shimmer of twenty-four-hour commerce. On the obsidian desk behind him, a solitary rectangle glows—his phone, pulsing with the silent urgency of a threat not yet spoken aloud. "The archive opens in 60 days. Choose what to protect."

He folds his arms, still, except for the subtle rhythm of his thumb against his wrist, silent as a metronome. He drinks in the city's spread—towers reflecting towers, circuit-board roads lit with traffic. Somewhere below, power and secrets sleep, or so the fools believe. The phone's luminosity paints his skin bone-pale and unblinking. Silas reads the message again, then once more, until every letter seems to hum with buried promise.

A cable of tension runs down his spine, yet the smile that ghosts across his mouth is almost indulgent. Some would panic, toss the device, call the lawyers and hackers and war-room strategists. He calculates. What currency will the archive unearth? Whose names and betrayals, whose shadowed deals will the storm drag into the sun? His mind sketches possibilities: the Brotherhood fracturing, or perhaps reforged, alliances burning down to steel. He closes his eyes for a moment, weighing futures as if they are code—lines of logic, recursive, tangled.

Beneath the plane of glass, the air tingles, faint scent of ozone seeping in through subtle cracks—there's a storm building out on the horizon, thunder a low suggestion behind the music of distant traffic. Silas wonders if tonight's rain will scrub the windows clean or mark them with the smoky aftermath of something scorched. The burdens he carries now are layered—leader, architect, silent brother-in-arms—but also older injuries, griefs he keeps sealed, stitched up beneath custom cuffs. There's always risk in secrets, he knows. Every encrypted archive is a ledger of sins, and when you inherit other people's debts, you never set the pace for their collection.

Still, some debts are his alone. His sister's laughter echoes, incongruous and sharp—memory flickers behind his eyes: the hospital corridor, the silence that came after. He learned then what loyalty costs. How it's paid in vigilance, in the silence between sentences, in the way you never let your guard drop fully. The countdown isn't a threat so much as a summons. It calls forth every ghost he's ever tried to bury beneath progress and acquisition, every truth he's shelved behind a polished reputation.

He's always trusted systems more than people. But the systems are showing cracks—helios infections, boardroom fractures, media campaigns that spin against the rules he once authored. He wonders, speculative and cold: When the archive opens, does daylight bring rot, or does it expose the groundwork for real renewal? Is legacy a fortress, or will it turn out to be a tomb?

His hand moves—deliberate, heavy-limbed—to pick up the phone. He dials a sequence known only to two people, his voice low and grained from disuse. "It's time to prepare. When the archive opens, nothing stays hidden. Not for any of us." Static answers; the other line listens. Silas doesn't repeat himself. The message, he knows, suffices.

In the hush after, Silas places the device face down, as if the secret lives inside the glass itself. He walks to the far wall, passing a shelf littered with awards earned in battles half-forgotten, stopping at a gallery of photographs—a timeline etched in pixels. A younger Silas, unsmiling, shaking hands with figures who later betrayed him. A news headline immortalized beside his sister's photo, haunting in its quiet pride. Low and steady, the hum of city powerlines joins the steady pit-pat of rain on glass. He stares at the faces, inspecting the grain of the prints. Each one, a choice. Each one, a reckoning not yet due.

His reflection hangs between the photos and the window—two versions of himself, split by transparency. The urge bubbles up to smash the glass, to let the storm in, to break his own carefully curated silence. Instead, he simply breathes.

A dialogue block forms in shadowed silence:

"Sixty days isn't long," the voice across the line says, distant, almost blurred by static.

"It's an eternity if you're waiting for the axe to fall. But it's enough if you're working. We'll move before the archive opens. We have to."

"There'll be casualties."

"There always are."

Silence falls between them—a contract signed in the absence of pleasantries.

He turns, flicks the lights off. The city dims around him, blue lightning slicing the cloudbank out beyond the window. On the desk, the phone's countdown glows like a radioactive wound, one secret tick disappearing every second. Silas lingers at the glass a moment longer, the taste of thunder rolling in the back of his throat. His silhouette merges with the night, a single motion in a world teetering on the edge of revelation.

Epilogue

The city was quiet after the storm.

For the first time in years, Orion Vega wasn't running. He stood in the penthouse living room with Elara's hand in his, Nova curled between them on the couch, her laughter a soft melody that chased away the ghosts. The world outside still whispered his name in scandal, but inside these walls, there was peace—fragile, hard-won, and more precious than any empire he had ever built.

He looked at Elara and knew: this was family. Not the one he had lost, but the one he had chosen. The one that had chosen him back.

But storms don't end forever.

On the glass coffee table, his phone buzzed once, then again. Across the city, in towers and boardrooms, every member of the Brotherhood received the same encrypted message:

"The archive opens in 60 days. Choose what to protect."

Orion's chest tightened. He met Elara's gaze—steady, unafraid—and saw the truth. Whatever came next, they would face it together.

Because storms could destroy.

But they could also cleanse.

And sometimes, they revealed who you were always meant to be.

Across town, in a tower of glass and steel, Silas Carver lowered his phone and stared out over the city lights. A faint smile curved his lips as he whispered into the empty room,

"The real storm is only beginning."

Final Thoughts

Every storm changes the world it touches. Orion's storm began in grief, spiraled into chaos, and nearly destroyed the fragile family he was desperate to keep. But in Elara's calm, he discovered something he never thought he deserved—love that demanded honesty, stability, and courage.

Together, they chose not perfection, but family. Not escape, but roots. And in Nova's laughter, Orion finally found redemption.

But storms never vanish completely. They shift. They build. They return. And as shadows close in on the Brotherhood, one truth remains: love makes them stronger, but secrets may yet tear them apart.

This is not the end. It is only the calm before the next storm.

Review Request

LOVED the Orion Dynasty Book Series?
Click here to leave your review on Amazon.

Your review helps this dark billionaire romance world reach new readers who crave power, passion, and redemption.
Or type this link into your browser:
https://www.amazon.com/review/create-review?asin=B0FSLM4W9K